"*Graffiti Girl* is exciting and romantic, and Angel is a strong heroine any girl can relate to."

—Allison van Diepen, author of *Snitch*

"[In her] edgy debut novel *Graffiti Girl*, Kelly Parra will surprise readers with her hip yet mature voice."

—RITA Award-winning author Dianna Love Snell

"Kelly Parra writes with the keen eye of an artist. *Graffiti Girl* is warm, gutsy, and true-to-life—an unflinching, honest portrayal of young adults. A seamless and impressive debut."

—Anne Frasier, *USA Today* bestselling author of *Garden of Darkness*

"Angel reminded me of myself as a young girl writing in California. Kelly, *felicidades* on your first novel; it's great to see Latinas writing positive novels about subjects that young people can relate to. I felt you weaved Angel's personal journey as a writer and growing young women with humor, realness, and craft."

—E-Fierce aka Elisha Miranda, author of *The Sista Hood: On the Mic*

Here's what Internet reviewers had to say about *Graffiti Girl*!

"Angel, in spite of her name, is one tough kid. Reading about her decision will captive the teen in us all. Get this one for the teenage girl in your life."

—Stacie Penney, on Raspberry-latte.blogspot.com

"*Graffiti Girl* was pretty awesome! I love the characters, especially Angel, and I was impressed with the way the difficult decisions Angel had to make were realistically fuzzy and grey rather than clearly black and white. . . . Fresh and interesting . . . Kelly Parra is an impressive new voice—keep an eye out!"

—TeensReadToo.com

"Amazing. This book could have come from the diary of a teenage girl."

—BookDivas.com

"Very raw, honest, and realistic, this novel portrays the Latino culture in a way I don't think I've seen before in YA literature. The events feel very real [and] lead up to a killer climax. I almost cried while reading this book. . . ."

—BookChic, on MySpace.com

"A colorful story, rich in art, culture, and human drama [and] an eye-opening lesson in the world of street graffiti. . . . Riveting, sad, and ultimately triumphant."

—Melissa, on MySpace.com

"Kelly Parra takes a look at cultural identity and peer pressure through the eyes of a sixteen-year-old named Angel. . . . *Graffiti Girl* will not inspire readers to deface property, but rather, to take pen to paper or paint to canvas."

—LittleWillow, on Slayground.livejournal.com/228066.html

Also by Kelly Parra

GRAFFITI GIRL

Available from MTV Books

INVISIBLE TOUCH
Kelly Parra

POCKET BOOKS   MTV BOOKS

New York   London   Toronto   Sydney

For my father, Manny,
and for Uncle Art, my Godfather.
You are both greatly missed by us all.

POCKET BOOKS
A Division of Simon & Schuster, Inc.
1230 Avenue of the Americas
New York, NY 10020

First MTV Books/Pocket Books trade paperback edition October 2008

Library of Congress Cataloging-in-Publication Data is available.

ISBN-13: 978-1-4165-6337-2
ISBN-10:   1-4165-6337-7

Acknowledgments

Many thanks to the following people who have helped to bring this novel to life. . . .

Tina Ferraro, dear friend and partner in cyberchats, for the reads and support as I wrote this novel.

To my very cool agent, Kristin Nelson, who always encourages me to do my best.

And to Jennifer Heddle, thank you again for giving this story a home. Your thoughts have made this novel stronger. Thanks to Jamie Cerota for suggesting the title.

More gratitude to the other folks at Pocket Books: Lisa Litwack, Erica Feldon, Jane Elias, and to MTV, as well as those of you I haven't met, who have assisted with *Invisible Touch*.

To the lovely authors, Dianna Love and Jana DeLeon, who took the time to read parts of this book.

To Ryan Schroyer for letting me pick his brain on cyber-tips when this book was just a thought in my head.

Thank you to all my extended family, new readers, and blogger/myspace friends. Everyone's support has been phenomenal.

To Ethan, Evan, and Samantha, who put up with me as I wrote through the holidays, and are always there to share in my excitement with each book. I love you.

Finally, a special note to Ethan . . . I'm sorry for the dent in the Chevelle. It was an accident, I swear.

SECRET FATES:
The Sign Seer's Blog

The first time I saw a sign, I didn't understand what I was seeing. We all hear stories of people receiving some sort of sign that leads them to a choice. Well, the sign I got was different, and I never had a choice.

I've read that everyone has a sixth sense—that flash of intuition when you feel a bad vibe, or when you think about someone an instant before he calls. Not that that will be enough to convince you. I know how difficult it is to believe in something that everyone else doesn't. It's almost as if you have to overcome a fear, to be brave enough to break away from society's view of normal. I'm not that brave. Not anymore. I don't allow myself to appear unlike everyone else, even though I am.

Believe it or not, I'm just what the title of my blog is called . . . a sign seer.

Years ago, I tried to convince others that what I saw was real. The confession backfired badly. I learned a serious lesson, one that still follows me today like a dark shadow.

The signs started when I was younger. I died—flatlined—for several minutes. After I woke, everything seemed clearer, more in focus. I started seeing strange images in the weirdest places. A picture would appear on someone's chest area, like a small screen showing me a quick flick.

I have to admit there are bad moments when I wonder if I'm dreaming it all . . . the signs and visions no one else can see. Believe me, I've tried to stop seeing the signs—just ignoring them—but I can't. The signs are as much a part of me as the color of my eyes and my hair.

If I follow the signs correctly, they usually lead me to someone in trouble and I try to help. Not always the easiest task for a seventeen-year-old girl, but I do my best to keep my life as uncomplicated as possible by following a series of Life Rules. Like this one:

Life Rule: Don't ever be honest with anyone about my ability.

So I thought if I record my experiences here and use this blog as an outlet for all my pent-up secrets, I can be myself, if only cyberly.

Because truthfully, sometimes I don't even know who I am . . .

—Sign Seer

1. The Hidden Me

The silence in my bedroom stretched so thin, I could have sworn there was no one else in the world but me. But with one click of my computer mouse, I would share my deepest secret with millions of strangers who surfed the web.

And I would do it anonymously.

Not written by Kara Martinez, a girl who did her best to appear normal, but the hidden girl who was far from normal and who no one else got to see.

The digital clock at the top of my screen read: 5:22 p.m. Mom would be home any minute.

I wet my lips and clicked "publish." Wiped my damp palms on my thighs and navigated to the homepage. I stared at my blog entry, reading it as if for the first time. As if I hadn't already agonized over every word, every sentence, a hundred times.

Above the blog, my website logo flowed in a thick, curving white font—"Secret Fates: The Sign Seer Blog"—against a black background. Next to the title was an ancient mirror with an image of a city scene in the center of the glass. A simple, clean design.

My straight hair fell forward like a veil on both sides of my face. I hooked the strands behind my ears before clicking to the browser homepage, clearing the history and the cache. Since launching the website two days ago, I'd taken every precaution to not leave any obvious connections between me and the website.

Thanks to plenty of online articles, I was as secure as I was going to be keeping my identity secret, unless I became the victim of a very determined and experienced hacker. At the moment, I wasn't on anyone's radar and was protected enough by security software that if someone tried to follow my ISP, I'd know it. I'd even gone a step further and signed on to an anonymous proxy by a software program that replaced my real IP address with a fake one, so that if anyone read my service logs, I'd be technically camouflaged. Being this cautious was the only way I would allow myself to have this website.

Just hoped I wouldn't end up regretting it.

I grabbed my now warm Coca-Cola cherry soda and took one last swig to finish it off. Tossed the can in my garbage tin and rolled my shoulders to stop the annoying itch at my back.

Done. No going back.

Standing, I pulled off my fitted black tee and threw it on

my bed, then picked up the pink top laid out on my pillows and slid it on.

The sudden low hum of the garage door from downstairs had me picking up speed to the oak-trimmed mirror above my dresser. My dark, shoulder-length hair was limp as usual. The soft beige of my complexion a little pale. Damn those dark circles under my eyes.

Tools of disguise were lined up across my dresser.

The brush came first, to quickly run it back through my tangled strands. A few dots of cover-up to smear on the darkness below my eyes. The gloss stick next—a swipe of pale pink across my mouth. I'd always wanted to try a darker maroon, but then thought better of it.

With my right hand, I smoothed down the soft material of the pink top. One of the many things Mom brought home after a trip to the mall.

I saw this at Mervyn's and knew it was you. You love pink.

I hadn't loved pink since the fourth grade.

Grabbing my discarded tee, I stuffed it in a plastic bag that I kept in my closet. My *other* laundry bag. The clothes I washed myself when Mom wasn't home. Then I grabbed the tall, thin silver thermos from my desk, the heat a comfort against my palm, and stashed it in a sandal shoe box.

One more quick mirror check—yep, the daughter my mother wanted me to be—and I headed downstairs.

The television was already turned on in the front room. A newscaster murmured the latest story at low volume. I strolled past, catching flashes of policemen and crime scene tape.

Another murder, gang related.

In the last three years, gang violence in Valdez, California (population 103,000), had boomed on the city streets. Even though an antigang task force had been formed in an attempt to stop street violence and schools were locked down when a gang rumble erupted, the task force hadn't stopped the gangs from retaliating against each other. After a while, you learned to live with the violence on the streets. Avoidance and playing it safe was the best defense, or so the police chief informed the public.

Safety was just an illusion maintained so that people could go about their lives. Danger and even death lurked behind every facet of life. Sad, but a reality I knew firsthand.

In the kitchen, Mom leaned against the gray stone counter, humming, while flipping through the mail. A brown leather briefcase stood at attention on the tiled floor. Her hair was styled in a simple yet elegant French twist, revealing her earlobes, dotted with tiny diamonds. A tailored light gray skirt and jacket fit her to perfection. Her blouse was white, and simple black two-inch pumps graced her petite feet. This was her business attire as a legal secretary at Stewart, Gerber & Mason Law.

If you didn't know Katherine Martinez, it was pretty much impossible to figure out she was half Mexican, since her Irish heritage prevailed. She didn't speak Spanish, although she understood it. And with her golden skin that could be mistaken for a suntan and reddish brown hair, she looked white. There wasn't even a hint she had a mother who was born and raised in Mexico.

Dad had been another story. Besides his dark skin and hair, Mexican roots had sprouted from him like blooming flowers, because, well, it simply had been who he was. The deep-down-to-the-heart part of him. He'd shared his heritage with his family in the food he cooked, the Spanish he spoke, and the stories he told of his childhood surrounded by aunts and uncles. With him gone, it was Mom's perfect "American" lifestyle that we now followed in this household.

Whether we liked it or not.

"Hey, Mom."

Mom glanced up with a smile, her humming coming to a pause. Her dark green eyes made their usual quick inspection; if everything *looked* normal with me, then everything was surely okay. Mom needed okay.

Life Rule: I needed Mom to feel okay.

"Hi, baby," she finally said with a relaxed smile.

I picked a red apple from the basket on the kitchen table, rubbing my thumb along the thick skin. Inspection passed. The tension in my shoulders eased. "What's for dinner?"

"Hmm. I'm thinking Chinese."

I'd been hoping for Mexican, as usual. I took a bite of the apple, chewed. "You read my mind. Beef broccoli sounds good."

"Heard from Jay?"

"No." A picture of him formed in my mind . . . a younger Jason, smiling. Happy. A time I remembered him best.

The lock on the front door rattled before Jason entered the house. I was used to the little occurrences of thinking of someone before they arrived or called on the phone, but that was as far as my "seeing" ability went with my family. I never came across signs that pertained to those I loved. Didn't know why. There wasn't exactly a Sign Seer Bible available for checkout at the local library.

Dark hair brushed the tops of Jason's brown eyes. He'd been blessed with these high cheekbones that made girls look twice, but the thick eyebrows and hard jawline he'd inherited from Dad stopped him from being too pretty. His clothes, worn a size too big, usually consisted of a T-shirt, faded jeans, Vans footwear, and a black zip-up hoodie.

"Hi, Jay," Mom said to him. "We were just talking about you."

He lifted his head in acknowledgment, his bangs clearing from his eyes, and loped his tall body straight to the fridge.

Mom turned and leaned against the counter, crossing her arms. "How was work?"

"Fine." Jason pulled out a soda can, shut the fridge, and popped the tab. The can retaliated with a quiet hiss.

"Good. We were thinking Chinese for dinner. Weren't we, Kara?"

"Yep," I answered, doing my part.

"What do you think, Jay?"

"Already ate," he managed before tipping his head back and chugging down the soda.

"Oh? What'd you have?" Mom's voice lost its cheerful tone. The forced smile she wore faded away. She knew we'd be having another dinner without my brother. It had been like that since he graduated from high school two years ago and started a job as an apprentice cameraman/errand boy at the local news station.

There were days I would have loved to yell, "Yo, Ma, wake up! Family dinners are history." But that wasn't who I was at home. I didn't express my opinions and did my best to keep the peace. Dad used to say Mom had a stubborn streak a mile wide. Oh, had he been right. Disagreeing with Mom was like going up against a brick wall bare-handed. You could hit at it, doing your best to break it down, but then you'd just end up with bruised hands, the wall still standing without a scratch.

All I knew about Jason's job was that he ran errands while he tried to learn about television. Not sure if that was what he wanted to do with his life. He didn't exactly share his aspirations with me. Well, the ass part of him came through just fine, actually.

"A burrito from a taqueria." He turned to leave the kitchen.

I sighed into my apple. *Lucky dog.*

"What are you up to now?" Mom wanted to know.

His shoulders slumped and he blew out a loud breath. I imagined his thick eyebrows lowering over his eyes in aggravation. "I'm grabbing a shower and change before I head out. Got an event to cover at the sports complex."

"When will you be home?"

He shook his head. "Probably around eleven. Don't

know." Then he was gone, and all we heard was the pounding of his footsteps up the carpeted staircase and his door slamming us out of his life.

I glanced at Mom. A faint wrinkle formed between her eyes, the rare hurt she let show, before she turned back to the mail, a comforting daily task.

Moments like these, I wished Dad were still alive.

2. My Fear

"**H**ere you go, Faith." I set a plastic bowl of milk outside the sliding door from the living room.

Faith, a thick-haired calico cat, purred under my stroking hand. I couldn't let her in the house since she shed hair everywhere, but Mom didn't object to keeping her in the backyard.

"Sleep tight." I slid the door closed, locked it, and shut off the patio light before returning to the kitchen table to finish my homework while Mom cleaned our already clean house. Instead of the low murmurings of the television, I heard the stereo in the front room, which was tuned to the classic rock station, with Sting singing about angel wings. Pretty ironic. Since Dad died—or in Mom's words, "was taken from us"— she didn't believe in angels, or even God, anymore.

I remembered the day I came home after the accident. The

two religious icons in our home had been taken down: the Palm Sunday leaves from above the front door, and the picture of the Virgin Mary from the living room. We even stopped attending the occasional Sunday mass. We hadn't been strict Catholics, but any religious roots we'd had vanished from our lives just like Dad.

Mom swept the floor and sponged the counters each night in case she missed a runaway germ the night before. Next, she'd go through the house and pick up anything out of place. On Sunday nights, she mopped the kitchen floor, dusted, and vacuumed each room in the house. It was rare for Mom to sit still for more than twenty minutes. Tonight was just Thursday, a surface-clean evening.

Spray counter, scrub counter. "Anything interesting happen today?"

Yeah, I wore all black, which you hate. And I posted my first blog entry on my new website about the thing I can never talk to you about.

I rolled the pencil between my thumb and middle finger. "Nothing out of the ordinary."

At dinner, we had gossiped about her work. It was amazing the kind of news that floated around an attorney's office. Now, as I finished up my homework, was when we usually talked about school.

Spray sink, scrub sink. "How's Danielle doing?"

"Fine."

Turn on faucet, rinse sink. "Good."

"Yeah," I said as I closed my history book. "Well, good night. I'm heading up."

"Okay, 'night, baby." She smiled at me before opening a top cupboard. "Sweet dreams."

I forced my lips to curve, gathered my stuff, and headed to the stairs. The stiffness in my neck was already relaxing.

"Kara?"

With my hand on the banister, I hesitated on the first step. "Yeah?"

"Did you use the last of the French vanilla?"

My fingers gripped the wood. "No." *Forgot to open the new coffee container.* "I, um, only have a cup every once in a while. I think you bought an extra can last week. Should be there."

"Oh, got it. Thanks."

My shoulders sagged. "Sure thing."

At the top of the staircase, I opened my bedroom door and dropped my books and binder in my purple book bag, then clicked on the small television in front of my bed. I slid open my drawers and pulled out some old gray sweats and a shirt with snoring pink bunnies on it, then stripped and changed. With a quick trip to the bathroom I shared with Jason, I washed up before heading back to my room.

A minute later there was a knock on my door.

Now what? A quick scan of my room told me everything was neat. "Yeah?"

Mom peeked in. "I may be home a little late tomorrow. Any plans?"

"I'll probably go watch a movie at Danielle's." I watched her look around my room. *Everything's clean.* No reason to come inside my room and start messing with things.

"Just call to check in after school and let me know for sure."

"All right," I said on a sigh. *Mistake.*

The final scrutiny of the evening: a quick study of my face. "Honey, are you sure you're okay?"

My pulse jumped, my posture straightening. "Mom, yeah, I'm fine."

She stepped into my room, crossing her arms across her chest. "You look a little tired." Mom's complete attention was like an eagle watching its prey. I felt like running and ducking for cover.

I gestured vaguely with my hand. "You know. It's the end of the day—"

"Have you been sleeping well?"

The back of my neck tingled. "*Yes.*"

She walked to my dresser, straightened my brush and my gel bottle on the corner edge. "I could give Dr. Hathaway a call."

No, no, no. I stepped forward and gave her a quick hug. The Estée Lauder perfume she always wore made my nose tingle. "Everything's perfect." *Believe me.*

She hugged me back, then leaned away. "Okay. But if you need me to call . . ."

"I'll let you know." *When I walk out of the house and see pigs fly.*

"Just don't stay up late watching television."

I nodded with a smile so hard, it felt as heavy as porcelain. "'Night." She turned and shut the door.

Letting the smile slip away, I grabbed my Rubik's Cube from my book bag and plopped onto my bed. Gripping the solidness of the plastic between my fingers, I turned the right column forward, flipped the cube over, looking for matching squares, rotating and twisting. A cube with fifty-four squares and six faces of color.

Simple, straightforward. Solid.

More than I could say for my own life.

I aligned one white row until I could feel that slow calmness come over me like spilled honey seeping through my body. A pocket of time passed until I heard the water running in Mom's master bathroom. I got up and pushed the lock on my knob, then sat in front of my computer and powered up, setting my cube aside. My knees bounced a steady rhythm as I signed on to an anonymous proxy. I couldn't help checking the website and statistics.

I scraped my teeth against my bottom lip. I should probably delete the blog. What was I thinking, blogging about my biggest secret?

The site was already listed on search engines, and my blog was registered with a blogging community. The statistics surprisingly showed six hits, visitors who had been directed to the site by accident.

I checked my blog entry. One comment.

Oh damn.

Stomach quivering, I clicked the hyperlink to read.

anonymous said . . .
are u for real?

I muffled a sudden laugh with my hand—a laugh so harsh it shook my shoulders, yet was somehow quiet and almost airless. It rumbled through me along with the tears building in my eyes. The tension inside me thinned . . . thinned . . . until it went away altogether.

With a hiccup, I typed the response: *Keep reading and find out.*

Okay, so I'd see how it went with the blog. Secret Fates was one small blog hidden among thousands, and I needed this. I needed an outlet. At first keeping the secret of the signs had felt good. I'd had something special to myself that not even Mom could take away. But as the years passed, keeping the signs a secret had started to chip away at my insides. I could feel myself drifting away into my own secret world that no one knew about.

I was afraid that one day, I might lose myself in that world forever.

The Secret Fates blog would hopefully keep that from happening.

I cleared the browser history and cache before shutting down, then stood to slide open my closet door. From the shoe box, I lifted the thermos I'd hid a couple of hours ago.

The first whiff of steam was wonderful as I poured hot French vanilla coffee into the plastic top. I turned off my lamp and, using the television as my only light source, gathered my iPod nano and inserted the earbuds. Sitting cross-legged, I selected my audio file, taking my first sip of the night.

"A large, big man . . . *un hombre grande,*" the woman's voice drifted into my ears.

"*Un hombre grande.*"

"A great man . . . *un gran hombre.*"

"*Un gran hombre,*" I whispered. "A great man."

3. First Sign

The day Dad died would be imprinted in my brain for the rest of my life. It was the day someone I loved with all I had was taken away. The day we lost the glue that had held the Martinez family together.

And the day I died for eleven minutes.

Somehow I wasn't sure this was what my English teacher, Mr. Taylor, meant as he rambled on about our new assignment to my fourth-period class.

"You're going to write about a moment in your life that really stood out to you." His small frame paced slowly in front of his desk like one of those ducks at a carnival shooting game. His short hair was combed neatly and his round glasses took up most of his face. "Good or bad. An event that may have changed something about you or affected someone close to you. Something . . . you'll never forget."

Words echoed in my mind . . .

Storm's coming in fast.

Daddy, I'm cold.

We're heading back now, mi'ja.

"The day I lost my virginity," someone mumbled from the back of the class, drawing out a couple of laughs.

I shifted in my seat, sliding the tip of my pencil eraser across my chin.

"You'll have three weeks to complete the essay," Mr. Taylor continued, unfazed. "A percentage of your quarter grade will be based on this paper. Make it count."

The bell rang and the movement of students filled the room. "Don't forget to do your reading assignment over the weekend," Mr. Taylor called out.

Danielle strolled to my desk, a smirk on her full lips. The green canvas bag hanging from her shoulder was spotted with patches and buttons. The bag matched her army-style coat, which she wore over a bright red fitted T-shirt and faded black overalls. Pen-marked Chuck Taylors covered her feet.

"Essays," she murmured. "The highlight of my life. Or more like the highlight of yours."

I smiled and grabbed my book bag. I happened to excel in English class. "Guess so."

"Pathetic. Why couldn't we use our pencils to draw images instead of words? I'd so ace this class then. Come on, let's go feed our faces."

We walked out into the pale yellow main hallway of kids

rushing off to eat or just hang out. The sounds of voices and slamming lockers vibrated against each other as we headed for our destination, the courtyard.

Neither of us had a car that we could use to take off at lunch. On her income, Mom couldn't afford another car after helping Jason to buy his used pickup, and I was slowly saving up. *Slowly* being the key word. Most of my money went toward my computer software programs and Secret Fates. Danielle didn't even have her license. She'd told me she didn't need one yet, which was true since she had two older siblings in college, one still living at home, who were fine with taking her places. If nothing else, Danielle was practical.

Danielle Salazar had been my perfect-for-me friend since my freshman year. She was petite, with long brown hair that curled past her shoulders. Pretty in that natural kind of way, but not enough to draw attention from any of the popular guys. She was an artist and, like me, hesitant about picking friends. She never caused trouble at school, got decent grades, and was polite to my mom. Maybe that's why we got along so well. We never made serious waves; instead, we cruised through life trying not to attract too much notice. We laughed, we joked, but we never spoke of the past. Sometimes not even the future, unless it involved Friday night plans.

As far as Danielle knew, my dad was dead, and she'd caught on early that was all I would say on the subject. Our friendship was far from normal, I knew. But it was steady, real, and the one relationship in my life I could always count on without any worries or problems. And in my life that meant a lot.

Stopping at our co-locker, I grabbed my coin purse and slipped it into my black jeans, stepping back for Danielle to perform her habitual search for her wallet.

"Got it," Danielle said. "I'm always losing this sucker." We stuffed our book bags inside the locker as best we could.

"I'm surprised you can find anything in that big bag of yours."

"For real." She slanted her eyes in my direction. "Quick— wallet in Spanish."

I hesitated, folding my lips in. "Oh, damn."

"Eehhh." Her irritating version of a buzzer. *"Wrong.* I told you how to say it before . . ."

"Um, *ca—capera?*"

"Cartera."

"I was close."

She did a quick eyebrow wiggle. "Not really."

"Ha-ha." My father had taught me the occasional Spanish phrase, but I'd never been fluent. And after his death, I didn't speak Spanish at all. At first it had hurt too much to try to remember, then it was like a giant force field holding back what little I had known in some dark crevice of my mind. Danielle was helping me bring back what I'd forgotten and hopefully more.

"So what's the daily lowdown?" Danielle wanted to know as we made our way to the courtyard.

Daily lowdown was our routine. We said we gossiped because it was fun. The real reason? It was a lot easier to talk about other people than our own lives.

"Not much. More rumors about Tiffany Jenkins getting down with some guy at a party."

Danielle rolled her eyes. "Too bad for her clueless boyfriend. I heard Kiley Weston is pregnant."

My eyebrows lifted. "Whoa, no way."

"All the way. That's why she's been gone for the past two weeks. Don't think she's coming back. Think her parents sent her off to some family home so she wouldn't embarrass them. Her dad's a doctor or something. Pretty crazy."

That hit a little too close to home. I cleared my throat. "Yeah."

The food court was packed with kids, and I swallowed hot air from the warm afternoon. Valdez High School was your typical diverse school with various nationalities and cliques. It was one of the first three high schools built in town, and with Valdez's growing population, there would soon be a fourth. Even with the crime, Valdez's population was steadily increasing, thanks in part to the large California Rodeo every summer, and neighboring Montecito—a popular tourist town—which had been written about in some literary classics.

I waited in line ahead of Danielle. A football player stood in front of me at the food window, which was strange since most senior jocks wouldn't be caught dead eating at school. Short blond hair teased the collar of his letterman jacket with the VHS Lions logo on the back. I only knew the names of a few of the football players—news of the most impressive plays traveled through school after a big game. Still, I didn't know who this guy was.

"Wait till you see Mr. Wallace's outfit today," Danielle said close to my ear.

I shifted sideways toward her. "Bad?"

"Oh no, the avocado suspenders go beautifully with the yellow tube socks."

I snorted. "I'm telling you, he owns nothing from after the seventies. I should know, I've watched *Dazed and Confused* a ton of times."

"You're just jealous because he wears those outfits to try and impress me."

"*Chica,* he's all yours."

"Come on," the football player said into the window, drawing my attention. "Meet me after school. Just to talk."

I didn't hear what the other person said, but apparently the two weren't seeing eye to eye.

"Don't worry about that, just meet me."

Danielle tapped me on the shoulder, then rolled her eyes. My lips twitched. Relationship drama.

Another player walked up to the front of the line. "Hey, Freddie, let's go, man."

Freddie Howards, then. Not just some high school football player, but *the* all-star quarterback of VHS. Definitely one of the players I didn't know in person, but everyone knew his name by reputation.

He lifted a hand to his friend as if to hold him off. "Are we cool?" he said to the person in the window.

He must have gotten what he wanted because he turned to face me.

I blinked and it happened.

As if I were standing beside a rushing train, the sounds of the courtyard heightened in my ears. Someone laughed loud and deep. The scrape of shoes on cement. Different voices assaulted my eardrums. Whispers. Shouts.

My mom grounded me for . . . How far did you get with her . . . Wicked, dude, when can I see . . .

The hairs on my arms raised. The pounding of my heart echoed in my head. My breathing slowed. Everything surrounding Freddie Howards faded away to pale gray. All I could see was Freddie; everything about him sharpened.

He has green eyes.

The color of a forest. The navy blue of his jacket brightened, the white leather covering his arms glowing. His skin was tanned and smooth. A few freckles were scattered across his high cheekbones. His lashes were as pale as his hair.

My eyes were helplessly drawn down his neck, past his Adam's apple and the collar of his shirt. Lower . . .

Right there on the chest of his open jacket, across his bright white T-shirt, an image formed, as if someone had clicked on a television screen. It was like watching a show with bad reception—flickering until the image became more focused.

"Gun," I whispered.

I blinked and everything flashed back to normal, the runaway train rushing past me. I clenched my hand into a fist to steady myself.

"What'd you say?" Freddie looked at me as if I'd spoken another language.

Life Rule: When caught acting weird, play dumb.

I let out the breath I'd been holding. "What?"

Danielle put a hand on my shoulder. "You okay?"

"Freddie, dude," the other football player said. "Let's go already."

Freddie shook his head with an irritated look and walked past me, his arm brushing against mine. Of course, I had to act as if everything was normal, that I hadn't really seen what I did. Lucky for me, acting normal when something was the complete opposite was as ingrained in me at this point as riding a bike.

I gave Danielle a shrug even as the hairs were still standing at attention on the back of my neck, and stepped up to the food window.

No one was there, just the lingering smell of fried food and grease. I leaned in and looked inside. People rushed around, filling orders.

One of the older cafeteria ladies walked in front of the window. "What'll it be?"

My attention zeroed in on the round, brown mole that protruded from her forehead. *You're not her.* "What happened to the other person who was here?"

"On break. Now, what do you want?"

That mole was so thick it actually shook while she talked. I tried not to cringe. "But who—"

"You're holding up the line, girl."

"Right. Pepperoni pizza slice and a Coke." I paid, snagged

my lunch, and stared out into the courtyard as I waited for Danielle. But I wasn't seeing the other students anymore. I was seeing the gun that had flashed before my eyes on the high school star quarterback.

I could already feel my palms dampening with nerves. My attention shifting from thinking about school and gossip to the sign. A dangerous one.

A new puzzle had begun.

In fifth period, I took out a blank note card and wrote in pencil . . .

Gun
F.H. (Arguing with someone to meet after school.)

If someone were to see that I wrote the word *gun,* they might freak out, but I knew I could pass it off as a note for a school report on violence. Truthfully, I was sort of freaking myself out. The sign of the gun on Freddie could mean anything. It could mean he owned a gun or knew someone who did. I worried about what it might really mean . . . that he was going to somehow be hurt or hurt someone with this type of weapon. The gun had looked like the weapons often used on television by law enforcement. Yet, considering this was the first piece of the puzzle, I couldn't jump to conclusions.

I took out my notebook and started a draft of my next blog entry . . .

Signs are just what they claim to be, images or objects you have to read in order to understand their meaning. The first signs I actually followed came to me at the age of twelve, and the first puzzle had been simple. I'd seen signs before my first puzzle, but I hadn't understood until then what I was supposed to do.

Not until one day in school, when I'd read a story about cats. Later, when I got home, I'd seen a television commercial about cats. Then Mom had come home, holding a magazine with a cat on the cover. When I went out to get something from Mom's car, a cat walked past me, an image of a car on its fur as it strolled into the street.

I heard a car coming. The cat had stopped in the street to lick its paws. I ran forward, stomping my feet. The cat startled and rushed to the sidewalk. The car missed it entirely.

From that day on, the cat stayed around the house until I finally named her and began to feed her each day. Back then I had thought the signs were all a coincidence, until it happened again. Then again. The signs showed themselves only once, though I sometimes saw them in altered forms later on.

With each puzzle, the details became a little more complex. Each time, the answer would end with me forced to help someone, or suffer guilt and headaches if I didn't try. Many times . . . either choice had the potential to turn out bad for myself.

Soon, I was finding lost items, knowing when someone was sick, preventing small disasters. And that was when I realized that the accident that had taken away my father had given me a gift.

An invisible gift that only I could see.

The problem was, a gift like this came with sacrifice and often emotional pain, sometimes making the ability feel like a curse. But ignoring my ability wasn't an option; the result would be more damage than I could handle. It was up to me to put the signs to good use.

—Sign Seer

4. Nancy Drew in Action

Danielle tugged at her curl, then wrapped the hair around her fingers. Released. Tugged. Rewrapped. "I just don't get why we're hanging around the parking lot. I don't want to spend the rest of my Friday here. Let's hang at my house. *Mi casa es su casa.*"

I ran my hand back through my hair. My scalp was sweating. "I know. Just a few minutes."

The air pushed, thick with heat. Valdez was experiencing an Indian summer, the sun scorching down on us when the leaves should be drifting orange and yellow from the trees. Next week it would probably be raining. I did my best to look inconspicuous standing next to the gated student parking lot.

"I'm checking something out," I told her.

"That's the thing—what?"

I finally spotted Freddie, walking with a couple of friends toward the parking lot. I quickly turned away, pretending to study the octagonal shapes in the fence that sectioned off the cars. I shut my eyes because sometimes I was a total dork. Could I be any smoother?

"Or is it who?" Danielle's tone changed. "Oh shit. Say it's not true. You *don't* have a crush on Freddie Howards?"

"*Shhh*," I said. "And no, I don't," I remembered to add.

"What happened at the lunch line—he zap you with his quarterback charm?"

I rolled my eyes.

She smiled. The smile said: *Poor, poor* chica. "Riiight. I mean, who hasn't crushed on him sometime in their poor pathetic life? He's hot, the high school quarterback. Hey, I heard he's got a wild streak, you know? Pretty much does what he wants, when he wants. Couldn't care less about the consequences. But the school lets him slide 'cause he's hot shit on the field." She sighed. "Man, he is so out of our league."

I lifted my eyebrows. "That's why I wouldn't waste my time."

She lifted her arm dramatically around us. "Yet, here we are . . ."

My lips twitched. "*So*, what else do you know about him?"

Danielle smirked. "Wouldn't you like to know."

Freddie gave a nod to his friend. "I'll catch you later at Dishes," he called out to him, and walked to his car, a four-door silver Blazer. He rested his arm on the roof, scanning the lot. His eyes skimmed over me and I shifted toward Danielle, who rolled her eyes.

"You're really good at this spying stuff, Nancy Drew."

"*Silencio*," I said without any heat. Discreetly, I looked in Freddie's direction. For the remainder of the lunch period, I'd watched the food line in hopes that the person who had been talking to Freddie would return. Hadn't happened.

Come on. Who are you supposed to meet?

Five minutes later, the parking lot was nearly empty and Freddie Howards was driving onto the street.

Whoever he'd been waiting for never showed. Again.

5. Unspoken Rule

Danielle was the youngest of three kids. Most days the Salazar household hummed with voices and chatter. When I visited—a couple of times a week—there were actual messes in the kitchen and living room, scattered books and magazines, shoes in various areas of the house. Not messy, but lived-in. Comfortable. A *real* family home.

Today wasn't any different. Muted rock music played from another room. The kitchen was bright with sky blue walls accented with red towels and porcelain decorative hens. The scent of microwave buttered popcorn drifted in the air.

Carmen, Danielle's older sister by two years, sat at the large oval kitchen table, munching on popcorn from a plate as she did homework. Books and notepads were piled in front of her. Carmen had long curls like Danielle, but her hair was the color of ebony. She was currently enrolled in the local junior college. Danielle's brother, Tomas, attended a university in Montecito and came home a few times a month for *familia* fixes, as he called them.

Carmen glanced at us. "Hey, Kara. Hey, brat."

"Hi," I said at the same time Danielle said, "Hey, punk."

Shifting my eyes toward Danielle, I nudged her hip with my own.

She looked at me.

I lifted my eyebrows.

The briefest of sighs passed her lips. She walked to the kitchen table, leaned against a chair, and stole some of her sister's popcorn. "Hey, Car . . . what are you doing later?"

"Probably hanging with Letty. Why?"

"Can you drop us at Dishes tonight?"

Dishes was this cool hamburger spot in the center of a big shopping complex that housed the mall and the movie theater. It served seriously huge burgers and waffle fries and housed a popular arcade area. After I'd heard Freddie would be there, I'd convinced Danielle to go. She still thought I had a crush on the quarterback and I wasn't going to let her think any different. I had a slight case of guilt for letting her believe it, but little white lies had been part of my life for so long, they were second nature. I kind of thought of them as sacrifice for a greater good.

"What time?" Carmen wanted to know.

"Around seven."

"Guess so."

"Gracias, muchacha bonita." Danielle grabbed more popcorn and a couple of kernels fell onto the table. "Next time get a bowl."

"No one did the dishes."

"Wasn't my turn," Danielle murmured.

Mrs. Salazar entered the kitchen from the garage. Latin music blasted behind her. She held a basket of laundry in her arms. Her black hair so dark you knew it had help was bunched at the back of her head. Stray curls fell around her brown face dotted with dark freckles. She was singing softly.

When she saw us, she smiled wide. *"Hola, mis chicas."*

"Hey, *mamá,*" Danielle said as I waved hello.

Mrs. Salazar was a stay-at-home mom, barely five feet tall, her figure voluptuously round. She liked to wear fitted jeans, peasant blouses in vivid colors, and lots of jewelry that jingled as she moved. She lugged the basket onto the kitchen table next to Carmen.

"*Mamá,* I'm doing homework here. Watch out for my popcorn."

"It's Friday. You have all weekend." She looked at me, winked. "My genius daughter. Thank goodness I have one girl around who is normal."

Danielle smiled. "Knew you loved me best, Ma."

"I'm talking about my adopted *chica,* Kara."

"Great." Danielle's voice was edged with sarcasm.

I laughed quietly. "Thanks, Mrs. Salazar."

Mrs. Salazar grinned, stepped to the kitchen counter, and opened a cupboard. Not a glass in sight. She leaned down and opened the dishwasher. "Who didn't run the dishwasher?"

I rubbed the tingle at the back of my neck.

I'll catch you later at Dishes.

No one did the dishes.

Who didn't run the dishwasher?

I knew not to ignore even the small signs around me, including something as subtle as repetitious words. In my experience, they often led to something important.

Life Rule: There are no such things as coincidences.

Danielle headed for the staircase. "Let's roll, *chica*." We walked up the carpeted steps to Danielle's room. The wall beside us was lined with family shots—pictures of Danielle, Carmen, and Tomas—all at various stages of their lives. Once we hit her room, Danielle dropped her book bag and fell straight back on her twin-size bed with a candy-striped comforter. I did the same and crawled next to her. Danielle scooted over to make room.

Posters and large pieces of artwork were pinned on her pale gray walls. A dark burgundy chair sat in one corner piled with clothes, a multicolored scarf, two purses, and a leather belt. Her dresser was white and dainty, like she'd had it since she was a little girl, which she probably had. Stickers and worn photographs lined the edges of the mirror. Next to the dresser stood a large drafting table with pens and pencils stuffed in a box, sketches scattered across the surface.

Danielle put pencil to paper and drew stunning images. I'd stopped telling her how talented she was. For some reason, she always brushed it off, as if she couldn't see what everyone else could.

Hands were her specialty. She drew them almost identical to her subject's. Some hands were simply drawn with the fingers spread. Others were posed in a gesture of emotion, such as hands fisted or giving an okay sign. Her favorite was taped next to her dresser, a girl's hand offering her middle finger. She'd even drawn mine, typing on a keyboard. She knew I was on a computer any chance I could get. The drawing was kept safe in a folder in my desk. I kept forgetting to get a frame for it. I wasn't allowed to tape or pin up pictures on my wall since Mom thought it looked tacky.

I shifted on my side of the bed. My body felt as light as air, as if I could float off at any moment. Wouldn't that be something, floating? Up, higher, maybe all the way to heaven . . .

Even though I was used to my lack of sleep, it often caught up to me at the end of the week, forcing me to rest even when I didn't want to. No matter what bad dreams lurked behind my closed eyes.

"I need sugar," Danielle murmured.

"Caffeine for me. Stay up late last night?"

She nodded, yawned. "Been working on a piece."

"Can I see?"

She pointed to the closet, then let her arm fall like a dead tree. I stood, ignoring the sluggish weight of my tired body, and slid open the door. A large drawing board was propped against another. I moved the top one to the side.

My eyes widened. "It's . . . wow."

On the board, a young girl sat in a darkened corner of a room. The walls were bare but for a window above her, showing the night sky and moon. She had her knees bent, her arms around them as she stared into the sky. So many variations of blue were smeared together like chalk. The design was as beautiful as most of Danielle's works. . . . but I connected with this one more than any of the others. The picture told a story of loneliness, something I knew well.

I never asked Danielle what inspired her to draw such lonely, dark pieces of art. Family surrounded her. She had both parents, happily married. But it was like an unspoken rule between us, we just didn't go below the surface of our friendship. We both knew we had secrets to keep and had enough respect for each other not to pry. Or was it that we didn't pry because we weren't ready to share our secrets with each other?

"I'm not done yet," Danielle said.

I swallowed. "It's really great."

"It's okay," she spoke quietly.

I glanced back at Danielle, expecting her to be looking at the picture. But she wasn't.

Her eyes, distant, stared out her bedroom window.

6. Dishes

A quick fix of soda and Snickers bars and Danielle and I were rejuvenated before Carmen dropped us off in front of Dishes around seven. The dark sky was spotted with gray clouds. A few stars peered through the clouds above us and it was hard not to stare up at the pretty sky.

A cold breeze rushed in from the coast a twenty-minute drive away. I shivered like I always did, thinking of how close I lived to the beach.

The one place I never would set foot again.

Rubbing my chilled arms over my thin sweater, I could see through the restaurant's windows that the place was already packed with customers.

"Now what?" Danielle asked. She wasn't thrilled about chasing after Freddie. Neither was I, but I couldn't really say that. Why else would I be looking for him if I didn't totally like the guy?

"We go in, try to get a table." Even I was surprised at how certain I sounded.

Except when we did go in, there were no empty tables.

"Thirty-minute wait," said the hostess.

Danielle tugged on the sleeve of my sweater. "Kara, let's blow this scene, just catch a movie. That new Ashton Kutcher flick looks hella funny."

I nearly gave in. Nearly. But the gun I'd seen on Freddie flashed in my mind like a lingering threat. It was like seeing an image behind my eyes. I shifted, rubbing my palm against a sudden low throb along my forehead.

Have to know what it means . . .

I scanned the dark arcade area connected to the left side of the restaurant and caught a glimpse of a navy blue and white jacket. "Let's not leave yet. Come on."

Squeezing through people in the arcade area, I lost sight of the jacket. My scalp itched. The accumulated body heat was intense. We settled in a darkened corner near a back-door exit and searched the crowd for the football player.

Why is it so hot in here?

"Don't think he's here," Danielle said, her tone beyond bored.

"He's here."

She went quiet.

I sighed. "I think he is . . ."

Danielle shifted beside me, leaning her weight to one side

and cocking her hip, pulling the zipper of her sweatshirt up. Down. Up again. "You know, Kara, you've never gone after a guy like this before. You must *really* have the hots for him."

I stared at a video game with Ms. Pac-Man puckering her bright red lips. "I'm not going *after* him."

She lifted her hand toward my face, fingers spread in a "stop" motion. "Whatever you got to tell yourself. Look for a few more minutes. I've got to use the porcelain god, then we'll take off. Okay?"

Taking a quick glance at her tired eyes, I relented. She hadn't wanted to come along, but she had for me. "Sure. But we should stick together."

Her lips twisted in a sarcastic smile. "Don't worry, *mi amiga,* I've been taking myself to the bathroom for a long time already. Know how to flush and everything." She threw me an exaggerated wink, then took off with a wave of her hand over her head before I could argue. Besides, what could I say? *I pictured a gun on Freddie earlier. It could mean something dangerous. And yeah, I'm as loco as I sound.*

Arms crossed, I craned my neck in order to see around people. Teenagers, adults, and little kids packed the arcade. Why had I thought it would be so simple to find Freddie in a crowd like this? I'd been hoping for another sign, something to tell me what to do next. Sometimes the signs came one after the other, other times days passed in between. Moments like these, when I didn't know what to do, I felt . . . helpless. Uneasy. And beneath the surface emotions—stupid, for pretending to have a crush on a guy I didn't even know.

The headache throbbed and crept around my head. A layer of perspiration formed above my lip. Irritated, I wiped the back of my hand against my mouth.

It was like my conscience was pushing me, but I didn't know why.

I never knew *why*.

Not until I solved the puzzle.

Someone bumped my shoulder as he moved by. I shot a glare at two Latino teens. The shaved heads, large white shirts, creased khaki pants were indications they claimed a rag color. The way they strutted in, chins tilted up like they didn't have anything to worry about, gave off a cocky vibe. Then again, in Valdez a lot of kids dressed like this, even acted like they were tough. It didn't mean the two gangbanged.

But if there was one thing I'd learned about following the signs, it was caution.

I watched them, hoping they were here to play games, then finally spotted Freddie and his friend at a video game across the room. The Latino guys walked in their direction. When they stopped behind Freddie, the back of my neck tingled.

One of the guys shoved Freddie from behind, and that was when I caught sight of the black flag hanging out of the other guy's back pocket.

My gut clenched.

Gang members.

Are they carrying?

Freddie and his friend whirled around. Already the duo

was toe-to-toe with the gangsters, pushing against each other's chests.

I stood rooted to my spot. I uncrossed my arms and clenched my hands at my sides, looking for someone to warn.

What do I do?

The gangster threw a punch into Freddie's face.

I flinched. Someone yelled.

The other football player and gang member crashed into a Mortal Kombat 2 video game.

Patrons scattered, blocking my view. I could no longer see the fight.

Danielle!

The bathrooms were located in the restaurant area. I pushed forward through a mob of bodies. Someone rammed into my side, an elbow knocking my chin. My teeth snapped together and I fell backward.

Arms caught me—someone bigger, stronger—and then I was pulled back through the exit door.

The distant raucous noise of the arcade became muted. Prickles danced along my face. The chilled evening air pressed against my cheeks. The arms loosened enough for me to scramble securely onto my feet and whirl around.

Instinctively I moved back, raising my head, breathing fast.

I blinked.

The rushing train came on so fast the world tilted. Intense sounds of my surroundings came first. The honk of a car horn rang against my eardrums. A cat's low, painful meow in the dark. Urgent voices from the patrons rushing out of the arcade.

Oh God, call the police . . . Mommy, I'm scared . . . Head for the car . . .

The pulse of my blood echoed in my head. My breaths thinned.

A guy—nineteen, twenty—stood in front of me, the street behind him fading to gray piece by piece, as if the world were a puzzle and he was the last part to complete it. His hazel eyes gleamed down at me with so many colors . . .

Brown, green, yellow, black.

His dark hair was cut short, but still long enough to show the beginning of untamed curls. Brown skin. Eyebrows thick. Eyelashes black and long. He was so intense looking. His mouth was in a flat line, as if he was angry that I was here with him. A thin scar cut through the middle of his top lip.

My eyes drifted lower, past his strong throat, his shoulders that seemed to be moving up and down at a slow pace. He wore a white ribbed tank top under an open black and gray flannel jacket. As I looked at his chest, expecting a sign, I . . . swallowed hard.

No image. There was . . .

Nothing but his tank top.

7. Mystery Guy

"*¿Está usted buena?*"

I blinked and all was quiet in my mind again.

"*¿Habla español?*"

I took a breath to try to calm myself. "I-I don't speak Spanish."

The guy stared down at me. "You all right?" His Spanish accent was gone.

"Yeah . . ."

"You sure?"

I'm not sure about anything. I went to step away, farther out of his reach, but then noticed he held on to my shoulders. He noticed too because he released me. His hands slipped into the front pockets of his jeans.

I looked around. A soft light above the door highlighted

the area. We were in an alleyway big enough for a car to drive through, the stink of the restaurant's Dumpster a few feet away.

The door shoved open and he pulled me away by tugging on my sweater. I stumbled closer into his personal space—close enough that I could feel his warmth. Smell his mild cologne.

People rushed out. Police sirens sounded in the distance.

Danielle.

Freddie.

I pivoted, ready to go back in. He pulled harder.

"You crazy?"

"My friend's in there."

"Not anymore. No one's there but who's throwing down. She's probably out front."

Think. "Okay. Thanks. For getting me out of there."

He gave a nod of his head. "Got to be careful these days."

A shiver ran down my back. "Yeah."

He stared at me for an uncomfortable few seconds as he studied my face. I broke away and started out of the alleyway. He walked beside me. We didn't speak.

It was incredibly strange to be walking next to him. A stranger, one I had *almost* seen with a sign. My mind replayed the moment I made eye contact with him, trying to understand the reaction I'd experienced. But it was all so muddled with the adrenaline rush of witnessing the fight in the arcade. He stood an entire head and a half taller than me, and was intense enough that just being near him made my heart race. I listened to our footsteps crunch against the asphalt and the tiny rocks that scattered.

A crowd had gathered in front of Dishes. Danielle stood off to the side, her head moving, searching the crowd.

I pointed. "There she is."

He said, "All right."

I caught Danielle's eye. She waved, and we started running toward each other. We hugged when we met. My heart was pounding.

"I'm so glad you're okay," I said. "I'm sorry we came here."

"It's okay." She pulled back. "We didn't know this would happen."

But in a way, I did know. The sign of a gun I'd seen on Freddie Howards had to have meant danger. And I brought Danielle along to find out more. I hadn't thought enough about her safety.

"What happened, Kara? Where'd you come from?"

"This guy . . ." I turned, scanning for him.

People. Cops. No sight of him.

"What guy?"

"I don't know."

A police car pulled to a stop, blue lights flashing. Another two close behind.

Two security guards attempted to nudge the curious customers back.

A guy in a suit, wearing a name tag, rushed to the policemen, hands pointed toward the restaurant.

I turned back and told her about Freddie and his friend

getting in the fight with the gangsters, and the mystery guy pulling me out the back. Just then the fire department and ambulance pulled into the mall lot.

"Do you think they were hurt bad?" Danielle asked.

"Not sure." I was pretty certain I hadn't heard gunshots, but it didn't mean anyone wasn't hurt. My fists tightened and I crossed my arms against my uneasy stomach. Was I supposed to have stopped this and I'd been too late?

Please don't let anyone be hurt.

Please don't let this be my fault . . .

I saw Freddie and his friend walk slowly out of Dishes. They were both pretty banged up. Blood dripped from Freddie's shoulder. He looked like he'd been cut.

But okay. My eyes closed for a quick moment.

The police had their guns out, yelling for them to get down.

Freddie spread his hands and did as demanded.

More policemen entered the restaurant.

But it didn't take my sixth sense to understand the gang members had likely gotten away, maybe through the same back door I had used.

A white vehicle sped into the lot, a news station van with KCBS 45 painted on the side. My brother's station. A cameraman stumbled out of the side door followed by Jason. A baseball cap was turned backward on his head.

I rubbed the silver loop in my ear between my fingers as I watched him. He was helping the crew with the cables and the microphone.

"Isn't that your brother?" Danielle asked.

"Yeah."

"Are you going to say something to him?"

"No."

"Oh-kay." She gave me a quick look like she wanted to say something more, but didn't. "I'll call for a ride." She stepped away and pulled out her cell phone.

Jason stared in Freddie's direction.

He finally scanned the scene and spotted me. His eyebrows lowered into a frown before he dropped his cables and jogged over to me. "What are you doing here?"

"Me and Danielle . . . came to eat."

He pointed his finger at me. "You better get home now. Mom finds out you were here—"

I looked down at the ground and shifted my stance. "We're leaving."

"Jason!" The cameraman called for him.

"Get out of here," he warned, and headed back to the news crew.

That night in my room, I took out my first note card and two fresh ones. Each note card stood for the signs I experienced.

Gun

F.H. (Arguing with someone to meet after school.)

F.H. (Gun aimed at him at Dishes by cops.)

On the second card, I wrote:

Dishes

F.H. (Fight with two gangsters, cut and beat-up.)

Mystery Guy (Pulled me to safety from fight. Felt as if I'd see a sign on him, but saw nothing.)

I laid both cards on my bed, side by side, and concentrated. And of course . . . nothing happened.

No flashing sign pointing to something important. That would have been too easy, wouldn't it?

I couldn't see any connection between these signs at all. The gun sign and the mystery guy could be from separate puzzles for all I knew. One thing I'd learned was that this ability didn't follow the kind of rules I tried to live by.

The mild headache was back, this time at my temples. With a sigh, I rubbed there with two fingers from each hand. From under my bed, I pulled out a shoe box loaded with packs of note cards rubber-banded together in various widths. Signs from my past.

I picked up one pack. The first card read "Forest Park." A neighbor had attempted a nature hike on a forest park trail and fell and broke his leg. If I hadn't found him, he could have gone into shock overnight. Another pack: "Peanuts." My ninth-grade teacher was severely allergic. She'd almost eaten a potluck dish that could have sent her to the hospital.

Next: "Fire." A leaking Bunsen burner that nearly caused a student to experience severe burns. But I'd stopped it from happening by sneaking out and sounding the fire alarm. Thank God I hadn't gotten caught for that one.

There were others . . . I hesitated on a single card labeled "Feather Man" and pushed it aside.

And now: "Gun."

What was I supposed to stop this time?

The headache spread from my temples like thick fingers across my forehead. I rubbed my face with both hands. Frustrated, I pushed off my bed and pulled a Red Bull from my sweatshirt pocket. One can gave me enough juice to stay awake for another few hours.

Opening the can, I sat cross-legged on the floor in front of the television.

The mystery guy flashed in my mind. His dark hair, his firm jawline, his stunning multicolored eyes. When would I meet him? Not if. There was no doubt in my mind we would cross paths again.

The thing that intrigued and even worried me most was the sign that never appeared on him. I'd experienced a similar reaction to someone only one time before.

I grabbed the "Feather Man" card from my bed.

The one puzzle I'd never been able to solve.

My eyes felt gritty, my body dead weight. I tried to swallow, but it was incredibly painful. I was in a bed, warm blankets on me. The lights in the room with the pale green walls were dim. A long curtain hung from the ceiling to my right. A television propped on the wall in front of me was turned off. I shifted to rub at my eyes and saw that a thin tube was connected to the back of my hand.

A man walked in front of the foot of my bed. He stopped and turned his attention toward me. Empty. No other word to describe the look in his eye. Then he continued on and walked straight through the door.

Fear hit me like a slap. My body jerked.

Mom! Dad!

I couldn't scream. I remained frozen. My chest hurt and tears sprung to my eyes. I saw a shadow move behind the current to my right.

Helplessly, I sat there, waiting for the shadow to move . . .

The curtain began to slowly slide open. I gripped the bed bars on either side of me.

The curtain slid all the way back and I couldn't move. I couldn't breathe . . .

I sat up in bed, sucking in air. Sweat leeched my nightshirt to my skin. Faded images were still in front of my eyes. As if glass figures moved around me, but I could barely make them out.

I spotted my television. My dresser. My bed. I was in *my* bed. Home.

Just a dream.

I rubbed my hands against my eyelids, then grabbed my Rubik's Cube from my nightstand. My hands shook a little. I licked my lips and sat back as I began to turn the mismatched squares.

SECRET FATES:
The Sign Seer's Blog

Before the signs began, I'd had an avid interest in puzzles. My father started me on solving brainteasers and riddles. He'd sit in front of the television on Sundays and do crosswords during the commercials while he watched football and baseball games. He'd hand the crossword back to me when the game resumed. I would work on it until the next set of commercials. Back then, I never thought my interest in puzzles would help me with where I am today. Or more to the point, with what I'm able to see today.

My dad taught me to look deeper when I was stuck on a puzzle, and other times to be patient for the next clue to reveal itself.

Yesterday was the beginning of another puzzle to solve. I saw a sign on a guy at school. Unfortunately, it was a sign of a gun. A gun could mean so many things. But I'm scared it could mean something harmful for someone. I just don't know who yet . . . or why.

Sometimes the why is the most important answer.

—Sign Seer

8. West Side

I met the mystery guy again at Papa John's.

Mom only allowed me to work weekend day and early evening shifts at the pizza place. Another rule I had to follow to keep her happy. It had been a struggle to get her to agree to a part-time job at all. When it came to me, she just wouldn't let her hold slacken. Dad was gone, Jason practically out the door, and I was the only one left for her to cling to. Add to that my past "problems," and she held on to me too tightly. But as long as I was under eighteen, I knew I had to hide my frustrations. For six more months, anyway. Even though I loved my mother, I feared the control she had over me. *The place she could send me* . . .

I was cleaning my last tables before the change of shifts when I heard the loud rumble of a car engine. I spotted him through the glass windows at a stoplight in front of the pizzeria.

The mystery guy from Dishes.

A customer called for her kid as the little boy ran past me, but I couldn't pull my eyes away from the mystery guy. He drove a black vintage car, a Chevelle with an SS emblem on the side. I would have recognized him anywhere, even with the black sunglasses. When he looked toward the pizzeria window, he saw me too. His lips curved into a half-smile.

A strange sensation tingled in my chest. I smiled in response. The traffic light changed to green and he looked forward and drove.

I thought of him and my surreal reaction to him last night. Someone else might think it was weird for me to see him again so soon, that maybe he'd followed me or something. But I knew better. Weird had been my friend since I was eleven.

Finishing my last table, I heard the same thunderous engine pull into the side parking lot. A few beats later, he walked through the door and toward me, his steps smooth and easy. My pulse sped up as I stood there holding two stacked pizza trays filled with paper plates, napkins, and four cups.

His hair was windblown and slightly wild, the black shades gone. He wore practically the same outfit I'd seen him in before, but this time with a black ribbed tank top minus the jacket, jeans, and what looked like black steel-toed boots. He was so nicely built, with rounded shoulders and a flat, toned stomach, it was hard not to stare. I caught a glimpse of a black ink tattoo on his left shoulder and wondered what the design was . . .

He scanned the restaurant, taking in who was there and where I worked all in one sweep. I itched to run my hand back through my hair, but both hands were gripped tightly to the pizza trays.

He looked at me, and it was as if his gaze held enough weight to press against the air. "How's it going?"

I shifted my stance from right foot to left. "Good."

His hands slid into the front pockets of his jeans, and he somehow shrugged at the same time. "So . . . what time you get off?"

"Now, actually."

He nodded. "Can we talk?"

Yeah, I wanted to talk to him, but what could he want to talk to me about? A nervous flutter tickled my gut. "Sure. Just let me . . ." I nodded toward the back.

"I'll wait outside." He turned and walked out the door.

I swallowed. And moved.

In a rush, I dumped my trays in back, grabbed my cell from my purse hanging in a locker, and dialed my brother's number.

"What?" I heard Jason say. Music blared in the background.

"It's me. I don't need a ride home."

"From where?"

I rolled my eyes. "You forgot about picking me up from work, didn't you?"

"Been busy."

"Well, I got it covered." Even if the mystery guy didn't drive me home, I'd catch a bus.

"Cool."

I dialed Mom's cell. She had asked Jason to pick me up since she had a working dinner. Her voice mail message came on, and I told her I was getting a ride home from Danielle's sister and going to her house for a while.

I peeked around the corner. He sat in his Chevelle, one arm stretched over the passenger seat. I punched out my time card and hurried into the bathroom, where I pulled off my apron and washed my hands, running my wet fingers through my hair.

My reflection stared back, my eyes wide, a hint of dark circles under them. I ignored the pink gloss in my purse and swiped my fingers under my eyes to fix my fading eyeliner. I wore my typical pizza outfit, fitted black tee and black jeans with my black tennis shoes. Lifting the hem of my shirt up to my nose, I sniffed.

Hope I don't smell too much like pepperoni.

My pulse sped up as I walked out the door, absently waving good-bye to the assistant manager.

I stepped out into the early evening light. The sun, still shining, had sunk lower in the sky. It had been hot all afternoon and now an early evening breeze cooled me. He leaned across his seat and shoved open the passenger door, then settled back.

I touched the frame of the car door and hesitated.

Cars drove by, radios blared, brakes squeaked. Nothing out of the ordinary happened. No sensations. No signs.

I didn't know a thing about this mystery guy. Not even his

name. I only knew that he'd kept me from getting hurt at the arcade. Somehow it was a comfort that he didn't know anything about me, my past, or my secrets—and that I didn't know his.

I told myself I was just following the signs, keeping my eyes open for anything that could help solve my newest puzzle, but the truth was I wanted to know more about him. I couldn't deny there were aspects beyond the signs that drew me to him. The way he seemed to know what went on around him. The way he watched me so intensely. It should've scared me, and maybe it did a little. I couldn't tell the future, yet I had a feeling something about mine involved him. The reasoning was just unclear.

I slid into his car and sat in the warm vinyl seat. The hood spread wide before me. It felt as if I were sitting in a tank.

"What's your name?" I finally asked.

"Anthony."

"I'm Kara."

His hand rested on the small padded steering wheel. "You want to go for a drive . . . Kara?"

I nodded. "Okay."

He slipped on the black shades, turned the ignition, and the car rumbled to life—like a gigantic, angry bear—giving me a little jolt. Rap music pulsed through the speakers. I set my tote purse on the floor between my feet and looked around for a seat belt.

Anthony reached across me and my stomach fluttered. I could smell that nice cologne on him as he pulled an old, bulky seat belt from the car floor and straightened it across my lap to secure me in. His fingers brushed my thigh. All I could do was sit quietly as he tightened the strap to fit me.

"All right?" he asked.

I swallowed and nodded.

He offered another half-smile before he pulled out of the parking space. That was when I noticed one faint dimple in his right cheek.

The car windows were midway down. Wind brushed my hair away from my face. Out of habit, I scanned the tall, ancient eucalyptus trees I'd seen all my life. The trees lined a large park and field. Long strips of bark scattered the ground. During winter, the West Coast was hit with harsh storms and reports of fallen trees traveled around town. Not long ago, a woman had been sitting in her car when a eucalyptus fell on the car. She'd died instantly. Danger lurked everywhere . . .

As if someone had tapped me on the shoulder to turn and look, I spotted the man with the feather hat, walking along the sidewalk. His mouth was shaped as if he whistled a tune. My fingers gripped the side of the seat.

Just like the trees, the Feather Man had been part of my childhood. I only knew about him what I'd seen with my own eyes. He usually wore cutoff shorts, cowboy boots, and a navy blue blazer. His skin was brown and aged. An overgrown black and gray beard and mustache covered most of his lower face. The cowboy hat was graced with a handful of various bird feathers: a turkey's, a blackbird's, possibly a seagull's.

The Feather Man haunted me every time I saw him walk the Valdez streets. My oldest unsolved mystery.

I turned forward and glanced at Anthony. Now I had two of them.

For a while, Anthony drove in silence. Since he had said he'd wanted to talk, I was content to follow his lead for a bit. He seemed comfortable with the quiet. The main road was spotted with cars. The sun would set soon, and there would be more locals cruising the streets.

Anthony lowered the radio. "Tell me something about you."

I see signs on people.

I looked straight ahead. "I'm not the greatest at sharing."

"That makes two of us."

It took me a moment to respond. "If I tell you about me, will you tell me something about you in return?"

One side of his mouth quirked up as he gave me a quick glance. "Sounds fair."

I combed my hand through my hair. "Well, I'm seventeen."

"Nineteen."

Surprised by his quick answer, I looked over at him. "I go to Valdez High."

"I don't."

I smiled. "I know."

"Don't go to school. Work."

I lifted my eyebrows. "I work at Papa John's pizzeria."

"J.J.'s car shop."

Will have to look that up. "I . . . have a brother."

"Same here," he said.

"I'm the youngest."

"Oldest."

"I'm mixed—Mexican-Irish."

"Mexican."

"Last night I was at Dishes, hanging out."

His hand flexed on the steering wheel. "The same."

I nodded, wondering if he was being completely honest. He didn't give off the impression he was a guy who hung out just for the hell of it. He seemed to be the type of guy who did everything for a reason.

"So," he said. "Why do I get the feeling you're telling me the answers that you want to know about me?"

"I don't know." I found myself trying to stop a laugh. "But that's the point of the game, right?"

His lips curved into a hint of a smile. "Clever."

He drove to the West Side of town. I rubbed my hand on my thigh. I didn't frequent the area. It was a place my mother drilled into my head to avoid since street crime had increased.

There wasn't a posted sign that separated one side of town from the other, but once you passed a long patch of open field and a creek, you just knew you were heading to the West Side, where homes were a little older and small markets had Spanish names like El Marketa and El Aguila.

"Where are we going?" I asked.

"Just driving. Nervous?"

I glanced at him. Had there been a little bite to his voice? I turned to look out the window without answering.

He pulled into a gas station. "Just need to fill up, then I'll take you home. Thirsty?"

I shook my head, even though I was. "No, thanks."

"Be right back." He got out and headed for the cashier.

A compact car was parked across. A couple of Mexican girls sat in the car, one in the front and another in the back passenger seat, windows down, with a third girl pumping gas. The two inside the car were talking loud and laughing. The girl in front had a tight ponytail, penciled-on brows, and heavy makeup.

She noticed me and her smile faded. "What are you looking at?"

I quickly looked down at my lap.

The girl in the backseat said, "Leave her alone, Josie."

Reaching for my tote, I pulled out my Rubik's Cube.

Josie laughed. "Tell her not to look at me, then." She called to me, "You're on the wrong side of town, mutt girl!" Then, more quietly, "Look whose car she's in."

Anthony rounded the hood of the car and handed me a bottle of cherry flavored cola through the open window. The tattoo on his left shoulder was of a coiled cobra ready to strike, drawn with black lines and shading. I hesitantly took the cold drink.

"You okay?" he asked. His shades were pushed up on his head and his eyes searched mine. He glanced at the cube on my lap.

I nodded and put the cube back in my tote.

"That your new *novia*, Anthony?"

He turned to the girls in the car. I heard him sigh. "A friend, Josie."

"Yeah, an *amiga* that don't belong in our neighborhood."

"How's it going, Dominique?" Anthony asked.

The girl in the backseat nodded her head, but seemed to be avoiding eye contact. "Good."

"Yeah, she's having a great time without Chico."

"Shut up, Josie," Dominique said.

Apparently Josie liked to laugh. A lot.

"All right, take it easy." Anthony walked to the pump.

The girl who had been pumping gas got back in the vehicle.

"Wait," Dominique said. "Let me grab some gum real quick."

Dominique pushed open the door and stepped out. She shut it and I blinked.

Sounds rushed together on high volume like water crashing through a drain. A cluster of music blasted from the street. The gas flowing into Anthony's gas tank echoed. A baby cried from a car seat. A car engine started. Voices surrounded me.

Fifteen dollars on four . . . Don't have that much . . . Get me a pack of cigs . . .

The car behind Dominique dulled to gray, her friends, the gas pump behind her.

Her dark eyes glowed brown.

She was slim, with long black hair that reached the middle of her back, her neck smooth and beige. The red of Dominique's blouse shined so bright. And on the front of her shirt, Freddie's gun flashed for my eyes only.

Only this time, the gun jerked with movement, firing two shots.

9. First Touch

"**K**ara, what's wrong?"

Anthony had sat beside me in the car again and I hadn't even noticed.

I swallowed past my dry mouth. "Nothing."

"You went pale for a second. Your eyes . . ."

I gripped the cold bottle in my hands.

"They say anything to you? If they did—"

"No. Not really."

"Josie's all talk. Been like that her whole life."

I looked at him. "You've known her that long?"

"She's my cousin."

Slowly, I turned the chilled bottle. "Oh."

"Kara, what's up?"

I hesitated. "If you didn't know me, would you know I wasn't from around here?"

He sat there for a second, then grabbed the key hanging from the ignition and started the car. "Yeah, I would."

The sun sank behind a horizon of houses. Anthony tossed his sunglasses on his dash, then drove out of the gas station without saying more.

"Well . . . why?" I pressed him.

From the corner of my eye, I saw him shrug. "The way you dress. Your hair."

Absently, I fingered my straight, thin hair.

"Your makeup. Even the way you walk. You don't have the attitude that comes from the streets." He paused. "You don't fit in here."

Then why did you bring me here? I guess it was a relief that it was the way I looked rather than something seeming odd about me. "Thanks for the drink," I said quietly. "How did you know?"

"Know what?"

"My favorite soda."

He glanced at me. "Lucky guess."

I gave Anthony directions to my house. The time on my cell was 6:47. The lights were still off, making the house appear empty and lonely. Relief settled through me, though, that I'd made it home before Mom.

Anthony pulled to the curb. The loud rumble of the engine shutting off made the neighborhood seem very quiet. The streetlight was two houses down, leaving us in the dark.

"Thanks for the drive," I said.

He nodded slowly. "Truthfully, I wanted to show you where I live. Where I'm from." He scanned my face. "Can I call you?"

I took in his serious expression in the dim lighting. *He wanted to show me where he was from before we started talking.* He was giving me a chance to decide whether I wanted to talk with someone from the West Side. If he'd only known it didn't matter to me where he lived.

I smiled. "Yeah. That'd be great."

"Let me see your cell a minute."

I handed him the phone. He flipped it open and dialed a number. Another cell started ringing. He pulled it from his pocket and answered, closed mine, then began to punch in numbers. He was saving my number to his phone.

A flutter began in my stomach at the possibility I would see him again.

He gave my phone back and I slipped it in my tote.

"Thanks again for the ride."

"Anytime." He leaned forward, hooked his fingers on my seat belt, his fingers brushing my thigh, and released the buckle.

I met his gaze. He still looked so serious. He lifted his hand and ran it down the back of my hair, then back up again to slide his thumb against the silver loop in my ear.

My pulse sped up.

"You're so delicate," he seemed to say to himself.

His thumb slid against the side of my jaw. His eyes drifted

to my mouth, then back to my eyes. My mouth felt dry and I swallowed.

"Good night, Kara," he said, and leaned back in his seat.

I nodded, a sense of disappointment shuddering through me. My head knew it was time to go, and yet a part of me wanted to stay.

"'Night," I barely whispered as I grabbed my soda and purse and slid out of the car. I swung the heavy door shut and waved before heading toward my house, digging my key out of my pocket.

When I got the front door open, I heard his engine rumble to life.

I turned on the front room light and shut the door, leaning against it. Listening to his loud engine fade away the farther he drove. I dropped my tote to the floor, gripping the bottle he'd given me. My heart beat so fast my chest was tingling. My fingers glided across my cheek where he'd touched me.

10. Mental Shield

I washed my personal laundry bag of favorite dark clothes and made a thermos of coffee before Mom returned home. I needed busywork to calm the emotions Anthony had stirred within me. Or, more accurately, cover them.

It was one of those safety reserves I had to have when faced with Mom. I would always love her, but I learned caution in every part of my life, with her being the top threat. I thought of the protection like slipping on a body of armor with a steel mask to match. Nothing would penetrate this mental shield and get to my real feelings beneath. Sometimes I even believed that.

An hour later, I sat with Mom at the kitchen table drinking coffee while she told me all about the dinner party she'd gone to that evening. When she kept trying to joke and laugh, I got this weird vibe, which caused the muscles in my shoulders to tighten. It wasn't her natural laugh.

Mom cleared her throat. "Oh, I got a call this afternoon . . ."

Here it comes. "Yeah, from who?"

"I don't want you to get upset, but . . . it was Dr. Hathaway."

My fingers clenched around the coffee cup. The cup had two teddy bears hugging each other, with the printed words: "I'm glad we have each other."

"You said you wouldn't call her unless I needed you to." My voice was a little sharp. *Chill out, Kara.* I took a breath to calm my agitation.

"I didn't." Her eyes widened as she sipped her coffee. She lied through her teeth. "She called to see how you were doing. It's been about a year since your last chat with her and she just wanted an update."

Ten months and twenty-one days, actually. My leg bounced under the table. "What did you tell her?"

"That you were doing well. I mentioned you seemed tired lately. She wondered if you were having any more nightmares."

"I told you I wasn't."

"I didn't know if you were being honest about it—"

"Why would I lie?" I asked, quietly, controlled. But I wanted to scream, *When are you going to just leave me alone?*

"So we went ahead and scheduled an appointment. Just a follow-up."

My stomach twisted. Last time was supposed to be the last follow-up. "When?"

"Monday morning."

The coffee in my stomach started to not feel so great. "Fine." I got up, took my cup to the kitchen sink.

"I know you aren't thrilled with this, but it's only because we're worried." She really meant *she* was worried. But she would never admit it. It was always "we" so she could feel she had someone on her side, or so I wouldn't just blame her alone. "You've been looking tired . . ."

With my back to her I said, "Okay, Mom." Not that I understood, because I didn't think I ever would. Just like she would never understand what was going on with me.

"It'll be fine," she said more to herself than to me.

"Yeah. See you in the morning."

I walked up the stairs when I wanted to run. *The mental shield isn't strong enough tonight.*

My stomach twisted and twisted, like threads of rope. Tightening. Knotting.

I grabbed pajamas and a towel from my room and strode to the hallway bathroom, locking the door. I turned on the shower, making the water hot, and flicked on the fan switch. I stripped my clothes as my heart pounded. I stepped into the hot spray, the heat rushing to my head. I felt dizzy and leaned against the tiled wall, holding my upset stomach.

The steam wouldn't let me breathe.

I sank to my knees and threw up light brown liquid.

Later, I was lying down in my room. My hand rested on my unsettled stomach as it made weird bubble noises. I couldn't sleep. Didn't want to. I didn't want to think about Monday and Dr. Hathaway. How I would have to convince her everything was fine so that she could leave me alone forever. I had naively thought I'd never have to face her again. I finally got up to add the girl Dominique to the "Gun" note card, then sat on the floor trying to connect the dots. My mind was too cluttered to focus.

I needed something.

Needed something other than the little world of my room.

I booted up my iMac to check my blog. I had two comments. One informed me: *If you want home insurance check out this site!* The other was by anonymous:

> anonymous said . . .
> who are u?

I felt too drained to feel irritated. I'd created a simple bio page without a photo, explaining I was a high school student who blogged anonymously about her psychic ability. Visitors either believed me or they didn't. I wasn't going to tell them who I was. I wasn't going to ever tell anyone. But at least anonymous was someone I could share my secrets with.

Placing my fingers to the keyboard, I responded:

> Sign Seer said . . .
> I'm just a girl.

And tonight I wished that more than anything. A girl who

didn't see signs. A girl who simply saw what everyone else did. A girl whose father was still alive . . .

I browsed a couple of my favorite blogs and decided to do a search on Anthony's workplace. I found a business listing, and the garage was legitimate. It also listed their employees, and one was named Anthony Garcia. I wrote down the address in case I needed it, and then checked my site once more.

Someone else had commented. I clicked on the link. A prickle at the back of my neck traveled straight up to my head.

anonymous said . . .
im going to find out which girl u are

11. Couch Doctor

"**S**till no memories of the boat accident?"

I shook my head. "None."

That was just my first lie of the session. I wondered how many I'd tally up in an hour.

My hand rubbed the arm of the paisley-covered chair. A soft lemony sent filled the room. It was probably supposed to be so subtle that patients couldn't smell it, but I always did. It was to the point that whenever I did smell the artificial lemon scent somewhere else, it brought me back here in my head.

Before I had started seeing Dr. Hathaway, I had this impression of therapy, leather couches and a bored, balding psychiatrist with glasses and a sweater vest.

Not this couch doctor.

Dr. Hathaway folded her hands in her lap. She had blond

hair wrapped in a bun that seemed to be fading in color each year. Her skin was pale and looked like paper—thin and smooth with a few crinkles. What I always remembered most about her were the dresses she wore, which looked as if they'd been the latest hot trend in 1982. Today's dress sported small pink roses on an ivory fabric, and an honest-to-God ruffle at the neck. Her shoes, of course, were very sensible, plain brown with a square heel.

"Your mother says you haven't been sleeping well."

"I told her I have been."

"Why do you think she would tell me otherwise?"

This was the thing about therapy. The questions were posed in a way to get you to say more than short sentences, in the hope that you and the doctor would eventually be led to the heart of your problems. Like, say, the death of my father? Or the truth she didn't know . . . how I was trapped inside my mother's grasp of what she considered sanity.

Have to be careful . . . "I don't know why she doesn't listen to me."

"She's concerned for you."

"I know."

Dr. Hathaway shifted in the chair across from me, crossing her right leg over her left thigh, causing the material of her dress to make a wispy sound.

"Kara, I've discussed a new treatment with your mother and now I want to present it to you."

My stomach fluttered. A new treatment? What was I, a guinea pig?

"You've probably seen on television the study of hypnosis?"

Someone get me out of here. I swallowed. "Yeah."

"Really it's about relaxing and a meditation state. A level of consciousness between awake and asleep. How would you feel about giving it a try?"

I flicked my eyes toward the door. "Why?"

Her thin, pastel lips stretched, her version of a smile. "I think you're blocking the traumatic experience of the boat accident. If you remember it and face it, I think it will help you sleep, move on to the normal life of a teenager. You were very young before, and I've been using this treatment with my older patients with successful results. I think you're ready to try something new."

My hand fisted. "My mother agreed to this?"

"She wants you to be happy, for the nightmares to go away." Dr. Hathaway glanced at my clenched hand.

Careful, remain calm. I spread out my fingers. "Well, no . . . I don't want to try it."

Dr. Hathaway's brow wrinkled. "Think about it. It can be frightening at first trying something new, but I can assure you it's safe."

I fidgeted in the chair, just wanting this hour to be over. "I don't think so. Thanks, anyway." *Why won't anybody listen to me?*

"What are you afraid of?"

"Spiders and snakes. Heights." *You.*

Dr. Hathaway smiled again. "Why are you afraid to try

the hypnosis? I would think it would be in your best interest to try and stop the nightmares."

"I told you, I don't have nightmares anymore."

Sure, it was a lie, but I had my own way of warding off bad dreams.

Staying awake as much as possible.

12. Farther Away

I slammed into the house through the garage door.

"Kara, slow down," Mom called out, trailing after me as I stalked up the stairs. "Stop, please."

Gripping the banister, I turned toward where she stood in the living room. Her purse was hooked in the crook of her arm. She wore another suit, this one with black slacks and matching jacket, and a silk bronze blouse. I wished I had the guts to ignore her completely, but who knew what she'd pull out of her bag of tricks if I did?

"It's only once a week for a month. What's it going to hurt?"

More like who. "I don't want to go. I'm fine. I wish you would just accept that."

"Then why wouldn't you agree to the hypnosis? Dr. Hathaway thinks maybe you're keeping something from us. That you're still having the nightmares."

And that I was hiding more than just the nightmares hung between us.

"I'm not, but you won't believe me." *You never will.* I continued up the stairs.

Jason stood on the landing, staring at me. His hands fisted at his sides. "You're seeing the doctor again?"

It could have been his tone of disbelief or the anger on his face, but for whatever reason, tears sprang to my eyes. I nodded as I moved past him.

I turned to close my door, but instead watched Jason rush down the stairs.

"Why are you making Kara go to that shrink again?" His voice was edged with accusation.

My grip tightened on the doorknob.

"Now you're suddenly interested in the family?"

"That's bull! She does not need doctors or drugs or a damn loony house."

"Don't use that tone with me, Jason. You have no idea what being a single parent is like. You—"

"I know what it's like to listen to my sister when she says she's not crazy. First the sessions—then what? Back to the hospital?"

I jerked back. Shock and gratitude shifted inside me. I couldn't remember the last time Jason had actually stuck up for me.

"Just stop! You're nineteen, it might seem like you know

everything, but you don't. I'm doing what's best for Kara. Just because she's getting some help doesn't mean she's crazy."

"You're only doing what's best for *you*."

"I'm the parent here, Jason. And this is my home. My responsibility."

"I'm not going to sit around and watch you put her through hell again."

I heard Jason pound up the stairs.

"*Jason!*" Mom yelled, coming up after him.

I swung open my door wider, watching my brother grab a duffel bag from his closet and stuff clothes in it. I squeezed the doorknob.

Mom stopped in his doorway. "What are you doing?"

"I'm outta here."

A shudder rushed through my body. My throat closed and tears streamed down my cheeks. My feet seemed frozen to the carpet, even though I wanted to slam the door shut and bury my head in my pillow to scream. *This can't be happening*.

"Jason, calm down. You don't have to leave." Mom's voice was still loud, but it lost the anger.

My gaze moved to the back of Mom's French twist. Smooth and perfect. *Mom, do something!*

Jason shook his head. "You won't listen to Kara, and you sure as hell won't listen to me."

He moved past her to the bathroom.

Mom followed, dogging his steps. "Where will you go?"

"I have friends." The medicine cabinet opened. Then shut.

"How very grown up of you, Jason."

"Whatever. I'll find my own place."

He walked back down the hall, his steps slowing when he saw me. His eyes flashed with something—it could have been pain—before he turned into his room, grabbed his jacket from his bed, and went down the stairs.

Mom walked to the top of the stairs, her arms folded against her chest. She had never settled down enough to put down her purse.

"Jason," she called out as he opened the front door.

I held my breath. She would do something to make everything right. To make him stay.

Jason stopped, but didn't look back at her. At us.

"Let me know where you end up staying. Please."

He nodded and left.

A heavy weight fell on me. So heavy, I leaned against the doorjamb of my bedroom. I felt like a cup that had been filled with so much sadness that any minute I would tip over from the burden of it all.

Both of us stood in the fragile silence; it felt like if we moved even a finger, something might come crashing down on us.

Then Mom walked down the steps and I . . .

I closed my door, let all that weight fall with me onto my bed, and cried.

SECRET FATES:
The Sign Seer's Blog

There's a serious downside to having this gift, and that's not being able to use it at will. Not being able to "see" something bad coming and feeling helpless as it all happens in front of me.

Sometimes I wish I didn't have this gift. Sometimes I wish it had happened to someone else. But then that would be wishing my pain on another person, and I don't think I could deal with that either.

I know all this probably doesn't make sense, but someone I care about moved further away from me today.

The worst thing about it is that it's my fault.

—Sign Seer

13. Candid

My emotions were numb the next day from having cried so much through the night. I felt like a worn sponge that had been squeezed dry. Hollow. Mom and I didn't talk much in the morning, other than to say good-bye. I couldn't stand to dwell on Jason's leaving or the guilt I felt for being the catalyst in his decision, so I did the only thing I could do.

This was one of the times I was grateful for my ability. Because when I felt I had nothing else to do but feel sorry for myself, I could shift my attentions to the latest signs.

Leaning against my locker, I shifted in my arms the bulky yearbook that I'd grabbed on my way out of the house. I didn't get very far following Freddie around, so I needed to try a new avenue. I glided my finger across the rows of pictures for last year's juniors. When a familiar wide face with silver braces came into view, I tapped the name.

Robert Benford.

The football player Freddie Howards had been tagging along with lately, and who'd also been in the fight at the arcade. I didn't know Robert, but I was pretty sure I knew his sister. Jennifer Benford. She was in my morning cooking class. Yeah, Mom didn't cook. Didn't mean I didn't want to learn the basics.

When I opened the locker to slip the yearbook inside, a square piece of paper fell to the floor. I automatically reached for it and realized it was a photograph.

A candid photo of Danielle and me with a couple of other kids as we stood in the lunch line. It looked like a picture for the yearbook or school paper taken during the first week of school. I couldn't remember it being shot. I flipped it over. No date.

"What is that?"

I jolted at Danielle's voice. Today her thick curls were bound back into a ponytail. She wore a green hoodie with a screen print of Shaggy on the front, with the phrase "Like, jeepers" printed over his head.

She reached for the photo, glancing at the book in my hands. "Is this for the yearbook?"

I shook my head. "I don't know."

"Hah. Look at me. I'm all giving a serious spaced-out look. You look good, though." She glanced at me. "What's up?"

I took the photo, shrugged. "Nothing."

She lifted her eyebrows. "Well, who gave it to you?"

"I just found it in the locker."

"Oh. Weird."

"Yeah."

She exchanged her textbook for another one in her locker. "Okay, catch you at fourth period."

"Yep." I stood there a moment longer, then slipped the photo in my binder and shut the locker.

Minutes later in the cooking room, I snagged a seat next to Jennifer Benford. Mrs. Nunes always chose partners seated close together. Baked nachos were on the agenda, easy prep. Jennifer cut triangles out of corn tortillas and I grated cheese.

Jennifer was a freshman with uneven brown hair that looked like she liked to chop it herself, and she wore a sweatshirt so big it fell to her knees.

"So, Jenny," I said. "Are you, like, related to Robert Benford?"

She rolled her eyes with a big smile. "My brother." She slanted me a look. "Why?"

"I've seen him hang with Freddie Howards . . ."

She nodded, with a sly smile. "He's *so* fine. I fan myself every time he comes to our house."

I gave a short laugh. "So does he have a girlfriend?"

"My brother or Freddie?"

"No offense against your brother, but Freddie. Not that I'd have a chance with him." I shrugged. "Just curious. I thought I saw him talking to some girl."

"As far as I know, he doesn't. Rob is always bragging how they play the field, and not just football."

"Are you sure?"

"Like I said, as far as I know."

Well, that's a dead end.

She smiled. "Maybe you will have a chance with him."

I smiled back. "Right. But a girl can dream."

I was stuck in the Freddie department and had no clue who he'd been talking to at the lunch line, or if that person even had anything to do with the gun puzzle. Then there was Dominique. Though I ran into her on the West Side with Anthony, I didn't know how she played into the puzzle or when I'd see her again. And who knew when or if Anthony would call me.

I glanced over at Danielle. We sat on the bleachers by the football field eating deli sandwiches. The sun shined down on us, making it almost too hot to eat. Well, I was the only one pretending to eat. Danielle held her sandwich in her lap. Her Chuck Taylors were propped up on the lower bench, her hoodie now tied around her waist. She stared at the field and it was as if she was miles away instead of right next to me.

Quiet moments like these with Danielle weren't unusual, but they were rare. I could have asked what was wrong. Could have said, "If you ever need to talk . . ." Could have emptied out my own family problems to her about my brother taking off. About my mom sending me back to the couch doctor.

But I knew neither of us wanted that.

Instead I bumped her shoulder with mine. "You're zoning out."

She flicked her attention back to her sandwich. "Yeah, my favorite pastime. Didn't you know?"

I hesitated over her quiet tone. "No daily lowdown?"

She shook her head. "Not today."

I cleared my throat. "So. I hung out with that guy from Dishes."

Danielle paused with the sandwich halfway to her mouth. "What guy?"

"You know, the one who pulled me out the back door."

Her eyebrows rose. "When?"

"Saturday."

"And you're just telling me now?" She said it in the sarcastic, joking tone she always used so I'd know she wasn't mad. And I was relieved she was back with me.

"Details, details, *chica*."

I smiled as I settled back into our regular routine, munching on my favorite jalepeño chips, then took a quick sip of my Coke to cool my tongue. "So he showed up at my work and we just went for a ride. Nothing spectacular."

"But what's he look like? Give me a name."

"Anthony . . . and he's kind of a tough guy." I shrugged. "Hot."

She flicked her eyes to my chips. "And we know how you like hot."

I laughed.

"Did you guys hook up or what? Get his number?"

"No, and yes."

She smiled. "What school does he go to?"

"Well, he's graduated. He's nineteen."

"An older guy, even. Look at you all dreamy. So I guess that leaves Freddie Howards out of the picture."

Terrific. I'd totally forgotten I was supposed to like him. "Yeah, my sights are set on a new man."

"You slut, you. I guess I'll have to meet this guy."

It was my turn to stare out into the distance. "Maybe you will."

14. Red Balloon

The late Tuesday afternoon sun blared down on me like a bright spotlight as I stepped off the bus. Black capri pants and a sleeveless gray tee weren't cool enough against the heat. I hooked my hair behind my ears, wishing I had a band to pull my hair off my neck. My tote purse and heavy school bag hung against my hip. I felt vulnerable walking on the sidewalk, watching cars drive by and feeling as if eyes were on me. The outsider on the West Side.

Even if Anthony hadn't flat-out told me how I didn't fit in his neighborhood, I would have known. It wasn't just my skin or my features that blended Mexican and white. Most of the females wore their hair especially long and thick. Mine was shoulder length, fine, and straight. The clothes on the locals were worn like a second skin by girls my age or baggy on the boys, and mine were neither.

I ignored the stares from men as I walked, keeping my head down as I moved past. I'd always been especially petite, with thin wrists and skinny ankles. And tended to catch the roaming eye of older men. Anthony had been right when he described me as fragile. I kept thinking how Mom would flip if she knew I was walking alone on the streets of the West Side. But I also knew someone would have to drag her kicking and screaming before she'd frequent this side of town.

The main road pulsed with activity. I passed a barbershop with two men sitting in chairs, smoking cigarettes. They wore brown slacks with cowboy boots and Western hats, speaking Spanish so thick I couldn't understand most of their words. A small vegetable stand was crowded with patrons choosing vegetables and fruit displayed on Mexican blankets. Spanish music played from inside the market and was drowned out by the passing lowrider cars, slammed to the ground, with music booming through the windows.

Wiping my damp forehead with the back my hand, I slipped the directions from the Internet out of my pocket and made sure I turned down the right side street.

It was a risk, going to Anthony's shop. I knew it. We hadn't talked since Saturday.

I wish I could say I was only making this surprise trip for the puzzle, trying to catch a glimpse of Dominique, but I'd just be fooling myself.

Anthony made me feel . . . just *feel,* and after all these uncontrollable things happening—the new sessions with Dr. Hathaway, Jason moving out—I wanted to take a step on my own instead of someone taking another step away from me or for me.

I didn't even know or care if that made sense.

The garage wasn't exactly big. It was located on a corner lot with two sliding-door car garages and what looked like a small office. I saw him right away, moving from under a car on a board with wheels. He wore a one-piece coverall with the top folded down around his waist and a dirty tank top. A navy bandanna was tied around his head, like a pirate. The bandanna suited him.

I hesitated going over to him. What if he didn't want to see me again? What if he thought it too weird that I came by his work?

What if, what if.

He stood, turned his head, and spotted me. His eyes didn't flicker in surprise. His lips curved as he wiped his hands on a dirty rag and walked toward me. Would anything surprise him?

He tilted his head slightly. "Just in the neighborhood?"

I laughed, kind of nervous. "Yeah, something like that."

He smiled and hunched down a little . . .

. . . and kissed me lightly on the lips. His mouth was warm and soft.

If a mind could stutter, mine did.

"Good to see you," he said.

"You too." I reached up to touch the silver loop in my ear.

He pulled out his phone, checked the time. "I'm not off for another half hour."

"It's okay. I just wanted to see where you worked."

"Not much, but it pays. Hang out in the office. The air's cool in there."

"Okay."

Anthony watched me walk away, running the rag through his fingers. Cool air surrounded me as I stepped into the office, and it was as if my body sighed with relief. I sat in one of three creaky metal chairs, plopping my school bag and purse on the floor in between my feet, still unsettled about the all too brief kiss. And wondered what it meant. Did he kiss every girl he knew like that?

For a few minutes, I stared at the automotive parts posters, the grease-stained notes posted behind the counter. An electric fan moved side to side in the small room, making the notes on the wall flutter for a second, then settle.

My body was hot and lazy from the walk. I dug some change out of my tote and went to the Coke machine against the left wall. I chose the soda with the highest caffeine and sugar content, even though I didn't care for the taste as much. Mountain Dew. I sat back down and played Tetris on my phone while I waited.

Time passed as I finished my drink and finally Anthony entered the small office.

"You playing a game?" He nodded his head toward my phone. A clean white T-shirt stretched across his shoulders, yet was loose around his waist. His hair was a little damp, as if he'd just done a quick washup.

"Oh yeah, Tetris." I closed my phone and slid it in my bag.

He grabbed my school bag for me and took my hand in his to lead me out the door. "What's your record?"

"Um." I tried to clear my head from the feel of my hand cradled in his big one. "Level 8, 22,500."

His eyebrows lifted in challenge. "Bet you I could beat it."

The heat covered me like a blanket as we made our way to his car. He opened the passenger door for me, then rounded the hood to his seat, setting my school bag in the back. All his windows were already down.

"Sure, I'll take that bet." The seats were like heating pads. I fumbled with the large seat belt and like before, he helped me with the strap, brushing my thighs with his fingers.

"All right." He slid on his shades. "Hungry?"

"A little."

"For?"

"Whatever."

He started the engine, with a hint of a smile. "I know just the place."

As he turned a corner onto a main street, I spotted the Feather Man. He walked with a spray bottle, rags, and window wiper hanging from his belt.

I licked my lips, pulse fluttering. "Anthony, do you know that man?"

"Where?"

I pointed to the right.

"Him? Nah. Been walking the streets for a long time, though. You know him?"

I shook my head, frowning. "No."

The Feather Man and Anthony didn't know each other.

Knowing that didn't tell me why I experienced the same odd feeling that a sign was coming—yet not one appeared on either of them. I was beginning to think the two weren't connected at all. Maybe it was some weird psychic quirk.

Yeah, right.

Anthony pulled up to a stoplight. A car next to us revved its engine. I glanced over: a kid wearing a baseball hat driving an older model car. Not vintage like Anthony's.

"What kind of car is that?" I asked Anthony.

"Mustang. Eighty-five. Eighty-six." He gave a small smile. His hand gripped the gearshift beside him. "Hold on."

"What are you going to—"

The light switched to green. Anthony pushed his foot against the accelerator. The Chevelle sped off.

My body slammed back against the seat, hands gripping vinyl. Air rushed through the windows. My hair whipped around my face.

The Mustang kept up beside us.

My heart pounded, my mouth drying. The engine accelerating.

The boat bounced across the waves. The wind blew my hair back. The salty spray on my skin.

The Mustang reached a car in front of him and he had to pull back. Anthony slowed and revved his engine.

He glanced at me as he downshifted. "You okay?"

I blinked several times, trying to tame my hair back down. "That was crazy."

He smiled fully. Reckless. "But fun."

I laughed a little as my heart rate settled back to normal. "I think we might have different views on the topic."

"He's got a fast engine, but not a match for my 396."

"Your what?"

"My engine. Been beefing up this motor since I was sixteen."

I just nodded as he went on about big blocks, headers, and carburetors. It was pretty much a foreign language to me.

Thankfully, Anthony soon pulled into the lot of a small outdoor Mexican restaurant, sitting on the corner of the main road and a side street. Construction work had gutted sections of the side street in front of the restaurant. Wooden barricades surrounded the holes. Men were sealing the holes one by one with heavy slabs of steel and seemed to be cleaning up for the day. Anthony and I ordered and ate tacos at a picnic table. Perfect. I'd been craving *carne asada* tacos for weeks.

"Good tacos," he told me as we sat across from each other. "Like 'em?"

"Hmm, the best," I said, savoring each bite of grilled meat and spicy guacamole. *This* was authentic Mexican food. I had yet to discover a good place on my side of town worth my time and dollars.

He nodded, his lips tilting down for a second. I was pretty

sure he was trying not to laugh. "Didn't think you'd be able to handle the guacamole."

My forehead was already perspiring from it. "It's hot. But I like hot."

He chuckled. "Good to know."

I smiled. I hadn't seen Anthony laugh openly before. He either half smiled or chuckled. The chuckle was either a muffled laugh into the side of his fist or a quiet one that looked like a laugh but with very little sound. I wasn't sure if it was a habit to cover the scar on his mouth. The smile he'd given me after the race had been the only time I'd seen him smile all the way without hesitation or reserve. I was beginning to think it was a habit to tone down his smiles, and that small thing made him more real to me. The truth was, I'd been a little intimidated by him. He'd seemed almost too nice looking. Too unreachable. To know he wasn't as cool and detached as I thought made it easier to be comfortable around him.

A toddler's cry came from the table next to us. A mother sat with three children, a child of about eight, a toddler standing on a bench seat, and a baby in the mother's arms. I glanced at the toddler. She kept saying, "*Globo, globo!*"

"*Globo* . . . what is she saying?"

"Means balloon. Guess she wants one."

The little girl stood up on the bench and turned toward us. For a second, I went still.

Sounds collided. An engine revved from the street. The music blared from the restaurant. I heard the children laughing, crying, melding into an echoing sound. The sizzle of frying food.

Kara, I guess I know . . . Come tu taco . . . Número doce . . .

The child shined vibrant against the dullness that formed around her.

Her dark eyes glowed black.

Her hair was pulled into two long braids. She wore a green jumper and right in the center flashed . . .

"A red balloon," I said quietly.

"No, just balloon."

I cleared my throat and took a sip of soda. "Right. What were we talking about?"

He stared at me a moment, his eyebrows slightly pinched. "Mexican food. Guess I know your weakness. What just happened, Kara?"

My eyes widened. "What?"

"You got that look in your eyes again, like at the gas station that day. Are you feeling okay?"

"I'm fine." My gut quivered. I was usually so good at covering up my reactions to the signs. How could Anthony be so aware of me?

I forced a smile. "I don't get Mexican food much at home."

He continued to look at me, and for a split second I thought he wasn't going to let me change the subject. Finally he took a drink from his soda and said, "The mom cooks a lot?"

Relief settled within me. "Never."

His eyebrows lifted. "Your mom never cooks?"

"Salads. Sandwiches. But mainly, no." *Not since Dad died.*

A memory flashed for me. Dad standing at the stove, his hip cocked. He was cooking up tacos—and some bad jokes. He'd enjoyed cooking. One of his first jobs out of high school had been as a cook at a small restaurant. I'd loved Dad's tacos.

"What do you eat?"

I shrugged. "Takeout. Chinese, Italian, American, Japanese, Indian."

"Why not Mexican? Is your mom Mexican?"

"Yeah, half. I don't really know why." And I would likely never ask, but yeah, I had my theories. All of them involving Dad.

He shrugged. "It's not for everyone."

I straightened a little on the bench. Remembering Dad made me remember the signs. I needed to ask Anthony how he knew Dominique, the girl with the gun sign. She was somehow connected to Freddie.

Life Rule: Don't ignore the connections.

We were having such a good time. I almost didn't want to bring the signs between us now. For once I wanted just to be the girl with the guy, hanging out and having a good meal. But I wasn't that normal girl, as the red balloon sign had plainly reminded me.

I shifted against the bench seat. "So, how's Josie?"

Anthony wiped his mouth with a napkin. "All right."

"Her friend." I cleared my throat. "She's pretty."

"Who? Dominique?"

Nodding, I said, "I think that's her name."

"She's cool."

"So she's not family?"

"No," he said, and seemed to find great interest in the construction beside us.

I bit into my taco. Anthony obviously didn't like to talk much about other people. I could respect that. Even I knew Dominique wasn't any of my business, but I needed answers. Unfortunately, I wasn't going to get them from Anthony. Not today.

As we finished, he gathered our baskets. "I'll turn these in."

"Okay, thanks."

I swiveled around on the bench to look out toward the street. The heat had died down with an early evening breeze. The main street was active with cars, people going home from work. A man pushed a small cart with pictures of ice cream cones on the side and rang a bell.

A sign of a red balloon.

What could it mean? And then it was just there—a small balloon floated on the wind. Floating, turning, half deflated, across the sidewalk of the side road with the construction.

I stood.

The back of my neck tingled. I'd never get used to seeing something no one else could see until I saw it in real life. I could handle the signs, but seeing them—*really* seeing them—always gave me that first little jolt.

I didn't know what I would do as I walked toward the balloon. It would look weird if I chased it, but I wanted . . . to touch it.

Make sure it was real.

The wind shifted, causing the balloon to float out toward the road construction, taking with it my hopes that this sign had meant something more. I stopped when the little girl with the braids streaked past me.

Everything slowed in my head.

In the back of my mind, I was aware of the mother shouting for the child, the construction workers covering holes farther down the street.

I yelled for the girl to stop, and I moved.

Moved fast.

I reached out for the girl. The only thing I could grab hold of was the strap of her jumper. My fingers hooked through, but I was going too fast. I wrapped my arms around her, but couldn't stop.

We both slammed against the wooden barricade in front of the hole.

In a split second I looked down.

The hole was deep. A large pipe below.

We were falling—

An arm reached around me, grabbing me as I held on to the little girl, jerking us away from the hole. Against him.

Anthony.

"*Fuck.* Are you okay?"

The little girl cried as I held her. The mother was already beside us, pulling away the child, holding her.

"*Gracias, gracias,*" she said.

I just stared, trying not to tremble. Physically, I was fine. My nerves just felt as if I'd shoved them into an electrical socket. "That was close," I murmured to myself.

"Too close. Fuck."

I focused on Anthony, his skin now a shade paler. For the first time I was seeing him without that cool attitude that made him tough and just a little dangerous. He was seriously shaken. Something clenched in my chest.

He still held on to my waist. I placed a hand on his shoulder. "It's okay."

He met my eyes for one long serious moment.

What's he thinking?

It seemed he finally realized what he was doing, showing a vulnerable side. He cleared his throat, let go of me, and rolled his shoulders.

The construction workers ran toward us.

"You were fast," Anthony said.

"Thanks for being faster."

He nodded, and his eyes lit with a glimmer of humor. "Not a problem."

15. Confrontation

"I'm glad you came by my work." Anthony's arm stretched across the back of my seat, his finger drawing an invisible line down the side of my neck. "Besides the construction scare."

It was about six when he pulled to a stop a little ways past my house. Mom was working late.

"Me too."

"Took guts to ride the bus and walk the streets. My neighborhood's not as bad as everyone thinks, but I could tell it makes you uncomfortable being there."

I shrugged, knowing I wasn't ready to share how nervous I'd been.

"Maybe you shouldn't do it again."

I met his eyes, thinking he was just kidding, and then looked down at my lap, suddenly feeling awkward. *Serious.*

He wasn't joking. If I could've grabbed my Rubik's Cube out of my purse without looking like a head case, I would have.

"You don't want me to come back?" I pushed my hair behind my right ear and tried to shift it so that it was a veil for my left side. "That's fine."

"I liked it, Kara. It's just the neighborhood isn't always safe to outsiders, and I'm not just talking about the construction. I don't want you to get hurt."

Always the outsider.

He unlatched his belt, and did the same for me. I was almost used to the gesture. Then he opened his phone, pushed some buttons, and handed it to me.

His Tetris record: Level 9, 27,850.

My lips curved. He had already scored higher than me. "I could probably beat that."

"All right." He closed his phone and set it down on his tray. "I want to see you again." He lifted my chin with two fingers to meet his eyes. His lids were heavy, eyes serious.

"I'd like that."

He moved closer.

A tingle of anticipation zipped through my stomach. I leaned forward and he brushed his lips against mine. I closed my eyes, our noses brushed, and he pressed his mouth closer to deepen the kiss. I tasted the soda he'd brought from the restaurant, and a slight tangy flavor from the tacos. His hand moved down to my thigh, and I slid mine to his shoulder. He was warm even through his shirt.

He kissed me like no other boy had kissed me before.

Soft. Slow. As if I was someone he wanted. As if he cared about me. I could already feel something inside of me open for him. I knew it was too soon. Knew that I didn't know much about him. But my instinct told me I could trust him.

He pulled back, shifted his mouth.

I was lost as my pulse fluttered.

A shoe scraped on the sidewalk through the open window behind me. "What the hell, Kara?"

I jerked back from Anthony.

Jason opened the door, latched onto my upper arm, and practically pulled me from the car.

"Jason, stop!" I stumbled to the sidewalk, more in shock than fear. My knees stinging with a jolt of pain. I sprang to my feet, rubbing my dirty hands on my capris. *What are you doing?*

Jason stood beside me, hands fisted at his sides.

A moment later, Anthony stepped in front of me. "Don't touch her like that again," he said so quietly, sounding dangerous.

"You're the one that needs to get your hands off my sister."

Still staring at Jason, Anthony asked, "This your brother?"

"Yes," I said, and licked my lips. I stepped closer to both of them. They were about the same height, both wearing a T-shirt and jeans, but that was where the similarities ended. Jason was a little slimmer in the chest and waist. He'd been a basketball player in high school. Anthony was wider in the shoulders with more muscle, a build similar to a wrestler or a football player.

"Jason, you're acting crazy." I didn't get his anger or why he was suddenly interested my life. He was supposed to be moved out, and he'd been distant for so long. Now he was going to bat for me with Mom and butting into my personal life? "Anthony's my friend, relax."

"I don't care who he is. He's not welcome here."

I blinked in surprise. When had anybody not been welcome here? Did they somehow know each other?

"Don't touch her like that again," Anthony said.

"Don't even *think* about threatening me."

I wasn't sure who stepped closer, but a second later, they were too close. A nervous fluttering sprang into my chest and stomach, even in my fingertips.

"Stop, you guys. *Please, Jason.*"

"Just get him out of here, Kara," Jason demanded, as he finally turned and stomped off toward the house.

My mind raced with doubt and embarrassment. I gripped my hands together, then released them. "Anthony, I'm so sorry. I don't know . . . why." I shook my head.

"It's cool." But by the hardening of his jaw and the cold look he shot in the direction of the house, I knew it was far from cool.

I had this overwhelming urge to make sure he was okay with me. I didn't want him to leave and never come back. Even though I was nervous and unsure of what he was really feeling, I circled my fingers around his wrist. I couldn't wrap my fingers all the way around. His pulse flickered pretty fast.

"It doesn't matter what he says," I murmured.

He met my eyes and some of the tension left his face. "Good." He leaned down and gave me a quick kiss. "I'll call."

He circled the Chevelle and slid in. He pulled my book bag to the front and I grabbed it and my tote purse before shutting the door. Soon after, the engine rumbled to life. He was the first guy to stand up for me who wasn't related to me, and that made it even harder to see him drive away.

Even though he'd reassured me . . . I still wondered if I would see him again.

I hooked my school bag and my tote purse on my shoulders, crossed my arms tightly against my uneasy stomach, and started up the drive to the house. Jason's pickup was now parked in the driveway.

Yeah, I was pissed off at Jason. He had no right to treat Anthony like that, but when I saw him hauling out bulky garbage bags into his truck, the anger drained out of me, leaving me empty. He was taking more of his things.

"You're really going," I said to him.

"Yeah. Been a long time coming." His words were clipped.

I wanted to ask why. Why did he and Mom never really talk, except to argue? Why did he close himself off from the two of us in the last few years? But I hadn't felt close to Jason in a long time, and I knew he wouldn't tell me. I understood that Dad's death had affected us each in our own ways. But I don't think I'd ever understand why his death seemed to tear us apart, and why we never found a way to heal together in six long years.

He opened the driver's door and looked at me over the

roof. For some sentimental reason only sisters could under-stand, I knew I'd remember this picture of him in my head for a long time. The way the sun gleamed off his overgrown black hair. His shoulders were round and strong. His eyes squinted a little against the sun, his mouth in a somber flat line. I no-ticed for the first time a faint purplish mark on his neck.

My brother had turned into a man and I hadn't even taken the time to notice until now.

"So, where are you crashing?" I asked him.

"With some friends until I get my own place. I'll call Mom and let her know. Kara, stay away from that guy."

I stared at him. "Why, Jason?"

"He's bad news. Trust me."

I didn't respond. At the moment, I didn't care all that much that he wouldn't tell me more. All I could focus on was his leaving. The fragile bridge that connected our relationship felt like it had finally broken, leaving a huge gap between us for good.

"You have my cell . . . if you need me," he said.

My throat tightened again. If I needed him? I needed someone, but it hadn't been my mom or my brother in a long time. They just hadn't been there for me.

Jason slid into his seat, slammed the door, and started the engine. As he backed out of the driveway, he didn't bother to look my way again.

Maybe I hadn't been there for them, either.

16. The Warning

Even though this was the second night Jason had been gone, it still felt like he was just at work, and he'd be home in a few hours.

How long would it take until I was used to him being gone all the time?

The phone rang while I finished my homework at the kitchen table.

Mom answered it. "I'm glad you called. I noticed you took more of your things . . . Where are you staying?" She wrote down something on a pad of paper by the phone. "You know, you can come home anytime. We can work things out."

I strained to hear them, my fingers tight on my pencil.

"Jason . . . when?" Mom's voice sharpened. "Yes, I'll take

care of it. Just check in with me every couple of days, okay? This isn't easy for any of us. All right. Be safe."

Mom hung up the phone. She stayed there for a few moments and I wondered what was wrong. She finally pivoted and walked to the table where I sat. Her hands gripped the back of a kitchen chair.

I looked at her. A frown was lined on her forehead above her perfect brows, which were lightly traced with reddish brown eyebrow pencil.

I twirled my pencil. "Is everything okay?" What had Jason done now?

She zeroed in on my gaze. "Are you seeing some gangster?"

I swallowed. "What?"

"You heard me, Kara Marie."

"*No*, I'm not seeing a gangster. Is that what Jason said?" *So that was his problem with Anthony.*

"Then you're not dating anyone? Jason said he saw you with him outside the house."

"A friend gave me a ride home. He's *not* a gang member. I don't even know why Jason said that."

"He said he's seen him around town with his gang. Kara, I can't believe you are interested in someone like that."

"Like what? You haven't even seen him." I shut my book and started gathering my stuff.

"Are you saying he's not from the West Side?"

"What does where he lives have to do with anything?"

"Don't act like you don't know what I'm talking about. If Jason says he's some Mexican gang member or is friends with them, I don't want you seeing him. With what we go through in this town, the shootings, the violence, I can't *believe* you would risk being around someone like that."

The way she said *Mexican* always sounded like she forgot the part of her that was Mexican. Who the Martinez family was. Who Dad had been.

I gathered my homework. "He isn't a gang member." That was all I could bring myself to say, as my hopes for an open relationship with Anthony were crushed. Maybe I hadn't believed we could all sit down together at dinner, but I had hoped there wouldn't have to be another secret to hide from her. Something else to lie about.

"What's his name?"

"Anthony." My voice was flat.

"*Full* name."

I remembered what I pulled up on the website. "Anthony Garcia, okay?"

"Just cut your ties now, Kara. Besides, with you in therapy right now—"

I flinched before I could stop myself.

"—it's not a good idea to start a relationship." She walked away and up the stairs, her stride determined. Mom always liked to have the last word. And she always ended with a bang.

I stood there in the quiet of the kitchen, gripping my binder as I struggled to control the emotion that vibrated through my body. I wasn't even sure which emotion it was— anger, fear, helplessness . . .

All I knew was that I couldn't risk revealing it to my mother.

To anyone.

Emotions had become something like a dirty little secret. If I revealed them in this house, it backfired. If I was angry, sad, withdrawn, it always resulted in a call to Dr. Hathaway.

Hiding my emotions was like taking a piece of paper and crumbling it into a ball as tight and as small as I could, then stuffing it away in a secret hiding place.

My entire body felt stiff and tight. Some days were worse than others.

The refrigerator clicked on with a low hum. I slid down in my chair and shut my eyes. My muscles were clenched tight. I took a breath. *Calm down, Kara. Calm down.*

It didn't work. I went up to my room, but there was still an urgency inside me. *Do something.* I heard Mom in the shower and locked my door. Grabbing my phone, I called Anthony's cell.

The phone rang until his voice mail clicked on.

"Leave a message," he said.

I closed the phone, ran my fingers through my hair, and paced. Back and forth, again and again. For the first time, I noticed a new hot pink blouse on my pillow.

The latest surprise from Mom. As usual the top was too bright, too pink. It would draw attention in a heartbeat. I stared at the top for *one second . . . two seconds . . . three.*

Throwing my phone onto the bed, I whirled and opened

the door. My heart beat in my chest. I jogged down the hall and knocked on my mother's door.

"*Mom.*"

The door swung open, my mother frowning. "What is it? What's wrong?" She wore her silk robe the color of raspberries, her hair wrapped in a towel.

I took a breath. "I'm sorry about earlier. I didn't mean to argue." And I meant it. No matter how messed up our relationship could be, Mom was the only secure constant in my life. She was my safety net and I was hers. When we had no one else, we had each other. I didn't want to forget that.

She shook her head, but the tension smoothed out on her face. "It's okay."

We stepped forward and held on to each other.

"It's okay," she said, her voice soft.

I closed my eyes, relieved. Yeah, things were "okay" for this moment. But okay didn't include much. It didn't include Jason. Dr. Hathaway. Anthony.

Okay didn't cover much at all.

SECRET FATES:
The Sign Seer's Blog

I helped save a little girl today.

The sign of a balloon had flashed on her torso. One red, float-ing balloon. Having these flashes of signs are often compli-cated. Half the time, I find myself wondering if one sign is connected to some other problem or just part of a entirely new puzzle. So I turned away to think about the meaning, wonder-ing if it could be part of the gun puzzle I'd been working on.

But when I saw an actual red balloon floating before me, I didn't hesitate. I walked toward it.

The girl raced toward it too—straight past me toward danger. I tried to save her, nearly got hurt myself, and someone was there to help us both. After it was over, I realized this sign was a warning all on its own to help the girl from an unfortunate fate.

And I also realized something else. It hadn't been the first time this someone had been there to help me . . .

—Sign Seer

Tuesday, October 29

Someone asked me in the comments how it felt to know I saved someone from getting hurt or worse.

Truthfully, at first helping someone feels sort of surreal. You have to remember nobody knows about my gift, and each day I have to pretend the same. So the reality of acknowledging that I've saved someone is hard to grasp in private moments.

I'm all alone dealing with these visions. I gather only what I can from the Internet for answers. I've never met a psychic in my life and because I'm afraid to tell my secret, I probably never will.

And before anyone asks, yeah, it's a really lonely way to live.

—Sign Seer

17. Giant Hand

Anthony didn't call all week.

I was so used to disappointment that it wasn't even much of a shock. Maybe Jason really did scare Anthony away. We didn't know each other that well and he could be the type of guy who didn't want to deal with a bunch of problems. Didn't feel I was worth the tension that surrounded dating me.

But there was this knot in my chest I couldn't ignore. I had felt something for Anthony. The feelings for him were too new to understand, but something I had wanted to explore further. He had awoken new feelings in me. I would never admit it aloud, but it hurt that he hadn't felt the same way. A new kind of hurt that didn't involve family or friendship. A hurt that made me feel fragile. I hoped those feelings went away soon.

Maybe not seeing Anthony was for the best, since Mom had told me to stop seeing him. If I didn't risk breaking Mom's rules, everything worked out. That was what I tried to tell myself. That was the safe way.

Life still went on at home with just Mom and me. Jason checked in every couple of days like he'd been asked to do. I tried to ignore the feeling that something was off, not complete. Such as the gun puzzle.

The feeling was there, like an itch that couldn't be appeased. The longer it was left unscratched the more irritating it grew, the more frustrating, until soon it became physically and mentally unbearable.

"What are they going to do?" Mom asked out loud. I didn't have to answer, this was how Mom watched television, with questions and remarks posed to thin air.

I sat on our forest green couch, a seat cushion between us, watching a crime investigation show, a matching couch pillow clutched to my chest. On the TV, the team was moving in on a terrorist threat, their elbows bent, Glocks out and pointed toward the sky.

More guns.

A sign or just coincidence?

"I knew it. They got away, didn't they?"

I hadn't gone looking for Freddie again. Since I hadn't talked to Anthony, I didn't have a connection to Dominique. I wasn't doing anything in the last few days to solve the signs.

I almost didn't care.

"If they don't save that poor guy soon . . ."

A headache pulsed at my temples and I winced.

I didn't get up. I just sat there and let the ache spread across my forehead like a giant hand. I shut my eyes and drifted . . .

Jason held my hand over the hospital bed rail. He was slouched in the chair when I shifted. My body was heavy. I felt so weak, groggy.

"Mom's getting some coffee," he said, his voice quick as if I'd start screaming again like I had when I first woke up.

"Jason . . ." My mouth was dry like paper. I licked my lips.

He scooted forward. "Yeah?"

"Something's different."

He stared at me without saying anything.

"Something's wrong. I saw—"

"Kara, its okay. Mom will be here in a minute."

"Dad. I need to see him."

Jason swallowed so hard, I noticed his Adam's apple move. He blinked a couple of times fast. "Just relax."

I shifted my fingers and gripped his hand a little tighter. "There was this man," I whispered. "He walked through the door."

His eyes widened. "What?"

"I'm scared. Don't know what it means. Dad—"

Jason pulled away from me. He stood so fast, his chair scraped against the hospital floor. "You—you were just dreaming. I'm getting Mom."

"Please don't go." My eyes watered.

After the door shut behind Jason, a woman so pale I could almost see through her entered my room.

My heart pounded. Tears streamed down my cheeks.

The door was still closed.

"Kara, wake up. Time for bed."

I blinked awake. My heart pounded fast. I rubbed my hands against the couch. Not a hospital bed. Mom stood next to the couch.

"You okay?" Her forehead was lined with concern.

The headache was still pounding, lurking.

"Fine." I got up and walked past her to the stairs.

"Good night," she said.

"'Night." When I made it to my room, I locked the door. Automatically, I went to my closet, but instead of opening it, I leaned my forehead against the door and shut my eyes.

Terrific.

I'd forgotten to make coffee.

Tonight I'd sleep. Tonight I'd dream. Whether I wanted to or not.

SECRET FATES:
The Sign Seer's Blog

I mentioned before that I couldn't ignore the signs. Ever since I nearly died, and the signs became apparent to me, I've suffered from headaches. The more I ignored the signs, the harsher the headaches became.

Pain relievers will work to a certain extent as long as I continue to follow the clues. But should I stray away from my ability, I pay a heavy price.

I try to look at it as a balance of the scales—the chronic pain comes with the signs, but when I help someone, the pain fades away for a time.

I *try* to look at it that way . . .

—Sign Seer

18. No Escape

My eyes felt gritty, like bits of sand were stuck behind my lids. Without the coffee to keep me awake, I'd tossed and turned all night, my head swimming with new images and old memories. I'd beaten back the headache with a couple of aspirin, and now it was a low whisper along my skull.

"You look a little out of it," Danielle told me in the morning. Little tiny clips held back the hair from her forehead.

I muffled a yawn with my hand, leaning against a locker. "Just need caffeine."

"We'll grab you a Coke at break. Are you up for something different tonight?"

I shrugged my shoulders. "Like what?"

She smiled. "Like I said, something different. *Un partido.*"

"A party? Whose?"

"Just one of Car's famous adventures."

Danielle's sister Carmen had been hitting the party scene ever since she got her Honda Civic at seventeen, and it seemed like she never had a dull moment.

"She's letting us tag along?" I snorted. "What brought that on?"

"I just decided to ask her."

With an embarrassed smile I said, "Thought of that one all by yourself, huh?" I kept forgetting Danielle and Carmen had a tighter bond than Jason and I. Sure, they teased each other, got on each other's nerves, but they never had a problem doing things together. Maybe it was a sisterly bond kind of a thing.

I finally said, "Guess so."

"Cool jewels, you can stay the night. I gotta jet." She strolled off to class.

I detoured to my locker before heading back to my own class. I stuffed one of the reading books inside and spotted a folded paper leaning against some textbooks.

I looked over my shoulder. No one around. I swiped the note and opened it. In black felt pen on a white background was simply . . .

I Know

The rest of the day flew by in a blur. I didn't feel really awake until night had fallen and we'd headed to the party. Kids were scattered on the lawn of the house. The front door was open and people drifted in and out. Music could be heard from the street.

The night felt as if it was full of something I couldn't understand. It was normal to feel a funny vibe when doing something new, even being somewhere new . . . but there was another feeling mixed in. Something irritating, something off. Wrong . . .

Could be because the party was on the West Side.

Being here made me think of Anthony, how he hadn't called, and I didn't want to think about him. Not tonight.

Danielle and I followed Carmen and her friend Letty into the house. Carmen wore fitted jeans and a red V-neck sweater, her ebony curls spilling down her back. Letty, wearing pretty much the same outfit, was a head shorter than Carmen, with dyed blond hair. Her brown roots gave her away.

Danielle and I didn't bother changing; we just freshened up. Jeans and sweatshirts were fine with us. Or as Danielle would say, "That's how we roll."

The house was ordinary, just some kid's home with the parents gone. And packed, packed with so many teens. I felt like that extra shirt trying to be squeezed into the already stuffed drawer.

Guys glanced at us. Some looked away. Some lingered. Girls gave us dirty looks. A majority of the guys looked like gangsters with XXL clothes, a few with black flags hanging from back pockets. I made sure not to make eye contact or otherwise draw their attention.

Carmen and Letty wanted to drink. I'd probably have to drive us home.

"You want beer?" Danielle asked. Her dark eyes were a little wide with excitement. How did she feel about being here? I had to admit it was good to see her so animated.

I shook my head. "Go ahead. I'll be the designated driver."

She smiled. "You sure? I'll make Car stick with one beer."

"Definitely. I'll catch the next one." I just wasn't in the mood to drink.

Danielle headed for the keg. I started to follow when a hand grabbed my shoulder. My whole body tensed as I shifted toward the person.

"I know you."

Freddie Howards.

What was he doing on the West Side? He'd gotten in a fight with those gangsters at Dishes. He was crazy to come to a party where he could be spotted and even jumped. Then I remembered Danielle's words.

I heard he's got a wild streak, you know? Pretty much does what he wants, when he wants. Couldn't care less about the consequences.

This was how it worked with the signs. Even if I didn't seek out more clues to the puzzles, the signs eventually found me. I should have realized there was a reason the headaches had been mild tonight.

Life Rule: You can never escape the signs.

Freddie leaned in close. His breath was mixed with liquor and mint. "You're that weird girl . . . who stares at me. Asks my friend's sister questions about me."

Embarrassment had me looking away. All I saw were faces I didn't know. Yeah, weird girl pretty much summed me up.

I tried to move, but he somehow maneuvered me against the wall, both of his arms caging me in.

"Jason's sister."

My heart beat fast as I zeroed in on his face. "You know my brother?"

His eyelids were low over bloodshot eyes. His cheeks flushed. "Why do you do that?"

I tried to push against the wall as much as I could, a useless attempt to add space between us. His face was so close. His eyes like gems cracked with red in the white of his eyes. His nose brushed my cheek. My stomach fluttered. I shifted my head away.

"Do what?" I asked.

He used his finger to turn my chin toward him, and his wet mouth brushed mine.

I jerked my head to the side. He was smashed if he was coming on to me. Freddie was likely used to girls falling at his feet. I wasn't one of them.

"Freddie, we're bailing." Robert Benford slapped a hand on his shoulder. Freddie blew me a kiss, then followed.

I closed my eyes, wiped a hand across my mouth, and sagged against the wall.

When I opened my eyes, I was staring at Anthony from across the room.

Everything inside me froze. I didn't speak. I didn't breathe. Then someone walked in front of him and broke our connection.

I inhaled and straightened, pushing my hair back away from my face. It was a useless gesture, since my hair just slid back against my warm cheeks. If only the wall could open up and swallow me whole.

He stood with a group of guys with shaved heads, some with black flags visible and proud. And even with his head full of hair, he fit in. He belonged.

I knew Anthony wasn't a gangster. Felt it in my gut.

A half-full bottle of beer dangled from his hand at his side. He started toward me and I crossed my arms. He stopped right in front of me, leaned in close.

His eyes burned into mine. "What the hell was that, Kara?"

19. Lost

An excuse lingered on the tip of my tongue. But Anthony hadn't called me in a week. I'd figured that whatever we had was pretty much done.

That maybe it had never even existed.

I stared into his hazel eyes and felt my rattled nerves seep away. This was Anthony. There wasn't anything to be scared about. He hadn't made me promises and I hadn't given any. He was a guy I'd met, and we'd kissed once. There hadn't been much more than that.

Liar, a voice whispered in my head.

"Nothing," I murmured, and shifted to walk away.

He put a hand on my shoulder. "Wait, Kara, let's talk."

I looked past him. There was so much activity in the house, but at the moment nothing could hold my attention.

The knot in my chest had returned. I didn't have the guts to face him right now. "Not now, Anthony."

I didn't want to hear excuses about why he'd stayed away from me. That really, I was just another girl to him. I knew the truth, hearing it out loud would be too much . . .

Just too much.

He ignored my objection. He moved his hand down my arm until he laced his fingers with mine and he pulled me toward the front door, bumping against other kids. Anthony's hand was warm and dry. Resigned, I didn't bother to struggle. I'd have to be strong enough to hear him out and then find Danielle so we could leave.

He led me out onto the sidewalk, about two houses down. The night was clear of clouds. Stars winked in the sky. But a strong breeze brushed against the trees, making the leaves rustle above us. One streetlight illuminated the area. His car was parked along the curb and I leaned against the passenger door. I hadn't noticed the Chevelle when we arrived, but I hadn't looked. Didn't think I'd run into him even if I was on his turf. Ignorance on my part.

He stood in front of me, beer still in hand. His hair had a little curl at the ends and over his ears; there was a slight shadow of whiskers above his upper lip. My stomach fluttered just looking at him, and that knot tightened. *How long did it take to stop liking someone? Weeks? . . . Months?*

"What were you doing with that chump? And what are you doing on this side of town at night?"

"I told you, nothing." I crossed my arms against the cold.

"He was drunk." I shrugged my shoulders. "It's none of your business."

"What do you mean none of my business?" He leaned in close. I could smell the beer on his breath. It was fresh. I didn't think he'd been drinking long. But I also smelled something familiar. His cologne and the guy scent that was just him. It made me want to get closer.

"I have to get back to my friend." I nudged him away. *Please, just let me get away from you.*

He placed one warm hand over mine on his chest. "Wait, Kara. I want to talk. Are you seeing him?"

His hand nearly swallowed mine. "I can't believe you're asking me this," I said.

He suddenly stepped away, shut his eyes, and took a breath. He looked at his beer, tightened his grip. I thought he was going to pitch the bottle down the street, but he tossed it in the gutter instead. Glass shattered. He started pacing in front of me, running his hand through his hair.

I pushed myself away from the fender, lifted my hands up in the air in a helpless gesture. "I can't talk right now."

Before I took two steps, he was in front of me. "Okay, all right." His hands cradled my face, his skin now cool. "Don't take off." His body gently pushed me against his car again. My body tingled. "I couldn't stand seeing someone else close to you."

I just shook my head. "Anthony, I don't understand."

"Kara . . ." He brushed his mouth on my forehead. "Damn, I've missed you."

I shut my eyes. The ground seemed to shift beneath my feet. *Then why,* I wanted to say. *Why haven't you called me?* But I couldn't bring myself to say it aloud. I was always afraid of hearing something I didn't want to, something that would be painful.

His hand cupped my cheek, and his lips brushed mine. "I don't want you with anyone else." Then his mouth opened mine for a deeper kiss.

The night was cold against my face, and Anthony's mouth was warm.

My arms wrapped around his waist inside his flannel jacket. His head shifted and the kiss changed. Became urgent, fast.

And like before, I was lost, lost in his kiss.

I never thought it possible for a kiss to take you away . . . until Anthony.

He broke away, resting his forehead against mine. We both took a moment to catch our breath.

"Be with me, Kara. Be my girl."

I swear my heart squeezed.

Deep inside, I'd wanted him to ask this, even though I didn't understand why he'd stayed away. Even without knowing if he would have called me again had I not seen him tonight. It just felt good to be with him. Right now, that's all that mattered.

"Yes," I whispered.

20. The Price

"**L**et me take you home." Anthony held my hand as we leaned against a wall in the living room of the party house, the side of his body warm against mine.

I shook my head. "Can't. I'm staying at Danielle's and I'm pretty sure I'm driving."

"All right." He looked around. "Damn, I don't see my brother. He was here earlier. You'll have to meet him sometime."

I smiled. "Sure."

Danielle said from behind me, "This is him, right?"

I shifted toward her. Danielle stood next to some tall guy, his eyes so low they looked like red slits. Her eyelids were just as lazy. *How much did she have to drink?*

"Yeah. Danielle, this is Anthony. Anthony, Danielle."

Danielle smiled. "Hey, mystery guy."

Anthony nodded his head, frowning a little.

"Ah," I said to him. "Inside joke."

Danielle lifted a thumb and pointed to the guy beside her. "This is . . . Barry."

He scratched his neck. "Larry," he muttered.

She took a swallow from her cup, then glanced at my hand holding Anthony's. "So, Car's ready to leave. She'll meet us at the car." She snorted. "Car's at the car. Get it?"

"Okay, yeah."

"I'll walk you out," Anthony said.

I smiled, then turned back to Danielle. Her mouth was glued to Larry's. It was such a surprise, I stared at them for a few seconds before I looked away. It was incredibly awkward to see someone's tongue shoved into someone else's mouth just a foot away.

Anthony lifted an eyebrow and gave me a small grin.

Danielle finally pulled back, shoving the guy's hands away really fast. Annoyance tightened her face. "Later."

"Hey," Larry said, swiping his hand across his mouth. "Can I, like, get your number?"

"In your dreams," she tossed back over her shoulder. "He kissed like a freakin' fish," she said to me.

I swallowed a laugh.

When I stepped outside, I noticed a large group of kids huddled together on the lawn. My stomach tightened, and my palms dampened. That uneasy feeling I'd had walking into the house came back full force. Like I'd been walking along and suddenly ran into a large spiderweb. No matter how much I tried to pull away, the sensation was still there stuck to me in bits and pieces.

We pushed our way forward, trying to get to the car.

"Oh shit," Danielle hissed. "It's Carmen!"

I pivoted toward the circle, rising on my toes. Carmen stood opposite another girl. Carmen's eyes were wide, her lips pressed tightly together, arms crossed against her chest.

The high ponytail of the other girl looked familiar.

I swallowed. Josie. Anthony's cousin.

Josie was up in Carmen's face. Letty stood by, biting her nails.

I didn't blame Letty for not getting involved. Josie wasn't somebody to mess with. She stood the same height as Carmen, except she had at least fifteen pounds on her. Carmen was slim, with a little extra weight in her back and chest. Josie had some muscle.

This wasn't our neighborhood. We all knew it. Now we were about to pay the price.

"That's my man you were hangin' all over!" Josie yelled. Her fists clenched at her sides. Her black halter top revealed her toned arms and thick waist. She'd already taken off her coat. She was pumped for a fight.

"He was hanging all over me," Carmen said.

"Fuckin' lyin' *puta*!" Josie shoved Carmen, and Carmen stumbled. She didn't push back. Josie's friends were all behind her. It wouldn't take much for them to jump in.

Danielle squeezed through the crowd. "Leave her alone!"

A couple of Josie's friends stepped closer.

I gripped Anthony's arm. *"Anthony . . ."*

"All right." He pushed his way forward. "Josie, chill out."

"She was on my *hombre*," Josie shouted. Her body visibly shook with pissed-off vibes.

Anthony looked over at a couple of guys leaning against a car so low to the ground it looked like it had no wheels. A black flag was folded neatly over one guy's shoulder. "Ricardo. Take care of this," Anthony said.

The guy, head shaved, a tattoo on his neck, jerked his head. He was laughing and holding out his arms. "Homie, I'm just mindin' my own business."

Josie moved fast. She grabbed Carmen's hair and lashed out with her fist.

I sucked in a breath. Danielle moved in, trying to grab for her sister, but the two girls crashed to the lawn.

Josie was on top, pounding with her fists. I'd seen wild animals on TV with more control.

Carmen helplessly blocked her face with her arms.

Kids hollered encouragement. "Damn, she's kicking that chick's ass," someone said to my right.

Anthony grabbed Josie around the waist, pulled her off of Carmen. The girl kept swinging, her legs kicking the air. "No! Lemme go! *Skanky-ass bitch!*"

I rushed forward and Danielle, Letty, and I helped Carmen to her feet. Her hair was a mess, her chest heaving. There was a red blotch beside her right eye. Her eyes were glossy with tears.

"Let's go," Danielle said, but all four of us already had the same idea.

We ushered Carmen across the street as fast as we could to the car. Josie's threats pierced the air like live ammo, and we all kept looking back as if we might get hit. Anthony was still trying to calm Josie down.

At that moment, the street dividing us felt like a mile wide.

21. Through Walls

My hands gripped the steering wheel. Headlights flashed into my eyes. The radio played so low I couldn't even tell what song was on.

All I could hear was Carmen's soft weeping.

Letty sat in the passenger seat, biting her nails. Danielle was in the back beside her sister, her arm wrapped around her shoulders.

When we were safely on the North Side, I pulled into a Denny's parking lot. Carmen needed to get cleaned up and under control before she went home.

Letty went to the bathroom with Carmen, while Danielle and I waited in a booth. We ordered hot chocolates and French fries.

I let out a relieved breath. "That was . . ."

"*Crazy.*"

"Will she be okay?"

Danielle nodded, twisting a strand of her hair. "Yeah, that bitch just scared her. She's never been in a fight before."

"Me neither. And Josie's scary."

Danielle's attention snapped to me. *"You know that psycho?"*

My stomach clenched. "Know of her. She's Anthony's cousin."

She stared. "You're kidding. And what, you like hang out with her?"

"No way." I shook my head and picked up a fork from the table to twirl it between my fingers.

"Kara, what are you getting into?"

I didn't look at her. "What do you mean?"

"Is Anthony a gangbanger?"

"No. Just because he's from the West Side doesn't mean he's in a gang." Even I knew my voice sounded defensive.

"But still, look what happened tonight. He's obviously caught up."

When Danielle said "caught up" she meant that Anthony had gang ties. That he was caught up in some kind of criminal lifestyle.

I met her gaze. Her eyes were red-rimmed from drinking, and her cheeks pale. "Danielle, it wasn't even my idea to go to a party over there, remember? I didn't know he'd be there, and we didn't know this would happen." For once, I could truthfully say that.

Being able to see the signs wasn't enough when I couldn't stop the bad things from happening to the people I cared about. I had no control over what the signs showed me. Never knew when they'd come. Never knew for certain what I was supposed to do. It was like being dealt a hand of cards and you just played them the best you could. Sometimes you won, and a lot of times you lost.

"Besides," I added. "Anthony *helped* Carmen."

Danielle slouched back in the booth, a tendril of hair falling against the side of her face. "I know." Her voice was quiet. "I didn't mean anything by it. It's just . . . a shock."

At first I thought she was referring to Carmen, but then she said, "I didn't even know you guys were serious, then suddenly he's just there, holding your hand."

I twisted the fork around. "I know. It happened fast."

"Are you guys together?"

I nodded. "He asked me tonight."

"Well, he's definitely fine."

My lips curved. "Yeah, he is." I lifted a shoulder. "And he's sweet to me." I looked at her. I wanted her to be okay with the relationship. She didn't have to be, and I'd still be with Anthony regardless, but I wanted Danielle to have my back. To understand and be accepting of the relationship when my family would never be.

Danielle finally smiled, and the stiffness in my shoulders relaxed.

"Wouldn't know he's sweet by looking at him," she said.

"I know."

"Just don't let him hurt you. Because if he does, he'll have to answer to me." She lifted her fist, pretty petite compared to Anthony's. "It may look small, but it packs a punch."

"Deal." I smiled. "Now you tell me what was up with you and that guy Larry."

"You mean Barry?"

"Yeah, whatever."

"Total fish mouth." She made an O shape with her lips and did this weird fish gesture where the circle grew smaller, then bigger.

I snorted out a laugh, even as I had the feeling she was trying to distract me. "Oh damn. That's funny."

She smiled. "Hey, I'm telling you. All true."

"But"—I cleared my throat, trying to stop the laugh from bubbling up again—"I've never seen you make out with a guy you didn't know before."

She shrugged. "First time for everything."

Still, it didn't seem like the girl I'd been hanging out with for two years. I didn't know how to say that to her without feeling like I was crossing that off-limits line that was never talked about but was always there between us.

Carmen and Letty started toward the table at the same time our food arrived.

"Keep it quiet about the psycho-bitch connection," Danielle whispered.

"Got it."

"The eye's not so bad," Danielle said to Carmen.

"Just a little puffy," I offered.

Carmen nodded and we all started eating.

My phone signaled a text message. I flipped it open. Anthony.

Anthony: cant talk. r u ok?

Me: yes. u?

Anthony: y. still chaos. call u ltr.

Me: k.

Anthony: ur on my mind.

Me: ur on mine 2. <3

Things had settled down by the time we reached Danielle's house. Surprisingly, Carmen confided in her mom about what happened at the party.

"Oh, *mi'ja,* I'm sorry." Mrs. Salazar took Carmen into her arms as Danielle, Letty, and I watched. "Does your eye hurt?"

"No. I just feel so stupid. I was just having fun, talking to a guy. I didn't know he had a girlfriend. And it was harmless flirting, *mamá.*"

Mrs. Salazar pushed Carmen's hair away from her face and tied it back with her hands like a ponytail. "It's not your fault. Sometimes we meet idiots in our life who only know how to solve conflict with their fists instead of with their minds. I'm glad you *niñas* stuck together. I think we learned a lesson here. No more parties on the West Side."

Everyone agreed, and I just sort of stared at Carmen and her mom. Mrs. Salazar's expression was soft with worry and sympathy. Carmen's face was open and sad. A girl comfortable with sharing anything with her mother, knowing she'd have her support no matter what.

Mrs. Salazar smiled at me, tilted her head. "You okay, Kara?"

Embarrassed, I nodded. "Fine."

"Let's crash, Kara," Danielle said, and I followed her up the stairs to her room.

I fell onto her bed, my body heavy with fatigue. "Your mom . . . she's, like, so understanding."

"Yeah." Danielle stripped off her top and pulled on a nightshirt. "She's pretty great."

"You could tell her anything."

Danielle jerked a shoulder. "Maybe not anything."

I raised my eyebrows. "No, but she wouldn't yell or stress out. She would just listen and say the right things. It must be cool to have a mom like that."

"Yeah, but Carmen doesn't know how to keep anything in. She shouldn't have told. Now my mom's going to go tell my dad and then she'll cry."

"What do you mean?"

"Anytime any of us gets hurt or upset, Mom feels it just as much. Maybe more. She goes and cries to my dad, and that hurts too. If it had happened to me, I wouldn't have brought it up."

I didn't say anything, but I understood where Danielle was coming from. Sometimes it was for the best not to share something that would cause a bad reaction. Safer.

We were quiet as we finished changing and made up a bed for me on the floor.

After we shut off the light and lay down, I could have sworn I heard Mrs. Salazar crying through the walls.

SECRET FATES:
The Sign Seer's Blog

You might be wondering what the accident was that somehow caused me to have my gift. Because of my anonymity I can't give away many details, but my heart was documented to have stopped for eleven minutes. I can't remember those eleven minutes at all. I can't confess to a white light or some encounter with a higher being. I don't really know why I was given this ability.

I will tell you that when I woke up, I saw ghosts. Walking spirits.

It took a while for me to figure this out. I was so out of it that I was beginning to think I was going crazy. I freaked out my family, and they tried to tell me I needed help. At first I believed them. I didn't want to see these scary people. I didn't want to be so different. I was terrified. During the second night of seeing the ghosts I cried, begging not to see them anymore. When I was checked out of the hospital soon after, I realized I no longer saw anyone who wasn't living and breathing. I was so relieved.

But when I stopped seeing the spirits, the signs began.

The first sign was a wrecked bicycle shown on a woman in her midtwenties. Seeing the signs the first time was too much to take. I started to hyperventilate and made myself faint.

I'm just sorry I didn't understand what I had been seeing. While riding her bike, the woman was hit by a car. The last I heard about her she was confined to a bed, maybe for the rest of her life.

—Sign Seer

22. One Truth

On Sunday, Anthony told me he wanted to take me someplace special. I told Mom I was working a full shift at the pizzeria. She complained. I nodded. She left to work out and Anthony picked me up four hours before my real shift.

He took the highway that skimmed along the Pacific Ocean. I'd driven by the ocean with Mom so many times over the past six years. From a distance, the waves always looked so wild and free and beautiful. The blue of the sky and the waves made it seem welcoming.

Up close and personal, those harsh, salty waves could be deadly.

When Anthony put on his blinker to turn in the direction of the beach, I swiveled my head toward him, my chest tightening. "What are you doing?"

He smiled. "I'm turning."

"No, I can't. I can't go here." My voice rose. A sudden pressure pushed against the center of my chest.

Anthony's brows pulled together as he turned. Traffic was behind us. "Why?"

"*I can't.* Just turn around. Please!"

Anthony reached one hand out to my knee. "Kara, calm down."

I covered my face with my hands. I started to tremble. "Take me home. *Please, Anthony.*"

"Kara, all right. Okay. I'm turning."

Anthony did take me home, just not to mine.

He said he wanted to talk.

I remained quiet. The pressure in my chest had eased, but the truth was, I wanted to be alone. I wanted to crawl into bed and not talk about what had just happened. I wanted to keep my past and problems hidden from him. Danielle knew I had secrets. I could tell. The difference was, she had secrets of her own, so we understood each other's need for privacy.

Anthony was in my life now, and in deeper than I'd ever thought possible. It was like there was a line we were going to cross, and if I wanted to keep him in my life, I wouldn't be able to keep some of my secrets.

How much would I tell him?

He lived on a small cul-de-sac called Fruit Circle. His house was faded blue, with white trim. He pulled into the driveway next to a tarp-covered car. Tall, bare rosebushes lined the front of the house like old soldiers trying to hang on. The lawn was neatly trimmed, but a little dry. Cars were parked along the circle of the cul-de-sac.

He held my hand as we went through the front door. An elderly man lounged in a recliner, watching TV. His hair was like white strings swept back across the crown of his head, his eyebrows thick and peppered with gray.

Anthony lifted a hand. *"Hola, abuelito."* Then to me, "My grandfather. He comes and watches cable at our house during the day."

The old man nodded his head, never taking his attention away from the Spanish television show.

Brown carpet, faded and worn, covered the hallway floor. Anthony pushed open a door to his room, shutting it behind us and pressing the knob lock.

I smelled a faint scent of his cologne in the air.

Car posters and pictures of girls in bathing suits were pinned on the white walls.

Anthony smiled at me. "Don't mind the posters."

A gray comforter covered his bed. He picked up a few pieces of clothing off the floor—a white T-shirt, black tank top, a pair of gray sweatpants—and threw them in his closet, sliding the door closed. "Have a seat." He motioned to the bed.

I sat down, hands gripped together on my lap.

"Want something to drink?"

I shook my head.

He went over to a small scratched table with a boom box on the surface, CDs piled to the side. He put on music, the volume low. Then he sat next to me close, but not close enough to touch.

I rubbed my palms on my knees to dry them.

"You want to tell me what happened back there?" he asked.

"Not really."

He made a quiet sound and took my hands in his. "It's okay, Kara. I'm not going to do anything but listen. I'm not going to judge you."

My eyes flicked to his. Held.

That was what I feared the most. If he found out the truth, he'd do what so many others had done in the past. Pass their judgment and walk away. Or worse, stay and think I was crazy.

I shifted my attention to the floor. An old carpet stain was about a foot away. Mom would have been on her hands and knees before she let a stain set into our floors.

Whether Anthony knew it or not, how he reacted about the accident would determine if our relationship stopped here or continued. If I shrugged it all off, closed off to him, he'd be disappointed. Maybe hurt.

Could I hurt Anthony?

I didn't want to find out.

I looked at my hands gripped tightly inside his. "Do you promise you won't tell anyone?"

He shifted and lifted one of my hands, fingers gripping the side of my palm, our thumbs crossing. A handshake of friendship. "You have my word."

A strange sensation bubbled up in my chest and began to spread like a flower blooming on fast-forward.

And I knew what it was . . .

Trust.

I swallowed past my dry mouth. "I was eleven when I went out on a friend's speedboat with my father."

Dark clouds hovered in the distance, but Dad had promised he'd take me for a quick ride before we had to return the boat to his friend. He hated to go back on a promise. Mom stayed home to do housework, and Jason hadn't wanted to go with us. He was mad at Dad about something and all he cared about were his video games. I knew he would have come with us to the ocean if he hadn't been mad.

"We'll only be able to make a quick run, *mi'ja*."

"Okay," I said with a smile. It was really cool to be with Dad all by myself.

The wind made his black hair whip around his brown face. Dark sunglasses covered his dark eyes. Like me, he wore a life vest over his faded blue T-shirt, with cutoff shorts. Everything Dad wore was faded. He even had the same jeans from years before. The only new clothing he owned came as gifts from me or Jason or Mom. He didn't shop for clothes. He spent money on taking us out to movies, eating out, or buying us things we wanted. Oh, and Lotto. That was Dad.

Once we were out a good distance, Dad drove the boat fast, leaving white ripples in our wake. The wind blew my hair back and made it hard to keep my eyes open. Salty water sprayed on my arms as I gripped onto the metal handle set into the side of the boat.

I glanced at Dad, and we both laughed. We had this connection. We could look at each other and it was as if we shared a secret joke. If there was humor in a situation, we found it. It drove Mom and Jason nuts.

Time flew by. I'm not sure how much. I hardly noticed the darkened skies had stretched over us until I felt the first fat raindrop hit my forehead. And then more. Soon I was drenched.

"Storm's coming in fast."

I shivered. "Daddy, I'm cold."

"We're heading back now, *mi'ja*."

Harsh rain slapped my face. I gripped the steel handle of the boat with both hands. Dad ripped off his sunglasses and raced the speedboat across the ocean water. The boat crashed up and down against the surface.

My teeth chattered. My stomach started to pitch from the rocky motion of the waves.

"Hold on, *mi'ja*!"

"I'm scared!"

Lightning flashed across the sky.

My pulse roared in my ears along with the rumble of thunder that vibrated above us in the boat. The rain pelted us like tiny rocks. I held tight to the handrail. Dad rushed us to the shore.

"No!" Dad yelled. "Damn it, hold on!"

And then we were in the air, tilting. My hands slid away from the handrail.

I screamed as I flew. Nothing but air surrounded me.

"Kara!"

I slammed into the ocean. Shock. Ice. Salt water clogged my mouth.

My arms struggled through thick, freezing water. Kelp tangled around my limbs. My life jacket forced me toward the surface.

Daddy!

"I woke up in a hospital bed." *Screaming. They said I'd been dead for eleven minutes.* "We'd collided with a bigger boat speeding to shore. My father . . ." I swallowed against the thickness in my throat. My neck and shoulders were stiff with tension. "He was the only one who didn't make it."

My head rested on Anthony's shoulder, his fingers rubbing back and forth on my neck. The gesture would have been comforting if I wasn't seeing that day so vividly in my mind.

This is where I stopped. I couldn't bring myself to say any more.

About the signs. The hospitals. The pitying looks.

My fingers were laced tight on my lap.

I felt Anthony shake his head. "Score one for Garcia. I couldn't have picked a worse place to take you."

His tone was light, and that fragile tension in the room began to melt away.

"Anthony . . . you didn't know."

He pulled away, and I lifted my head to look at him.

His hazel eyes were clear and focused. "Nothing can take away that kind of pain, Kara. I'm sorry."

"I never told anyone before." My voice was quiet. For a long time I couldn't even bring myself to remember the details, then when I did I couldn't tell anyone. Not Dr. Hathaway, my brother, or my mom. Not after I tried to tell them what I'd seen in the hospital when I first awoke after the accident, and no one believed me.

Of course, no one in his right mind would believe what I'd seen.

So why was I telling Anthony about the accident? Because it was easier to share secrets with someone you were just beginning to know. Because I wanted to be truthful to someone I cared about for once.

Because I trusted him.

Anthony looked at me for a long moment, then cleared his throat.

"I've never lost anyone in my family," he said. "But . . . about two years ago, I lost my best friend."

It was so unexpected, I didn't really know what to say.

"Me and Pedro, we grew up in the neighborhood, and we joined up with Las Cobras."

"You were part of a gang?"

His smile was grim. "You grow up here, it's part of your life. You make friends. Enemies. You need protection on the streets. It's a brotherhood. The messed-up part is the fights.

Retaliation. It's not about throwing down anymore. It's about shoving a gun in someone's face." He stood up, ran his fingers back through his hair.

"What happened?"

He looked at me. Shook his head.

"You don't have to tell me . . ."

His hands slid into his front jean pockets. His eyes shifted to his stereo, but I didn't think he was really seeing it. "There was a beef with a guy from another gang. Some dumb shit over staring down at a party. They threw down. Pedro kicked his ass. Two nights later, he got shot on the street."

I stood up, but didn't go to him. I laced my fingers together in front of me. Funny what a close relationship I had with grief, and how I still felt as awkward as the next person in the presence of someone else's. "I'm sorry."

"There were witnesses. The guy was arrested and locked up. After that, I was done bangin'."

"You just walked away?"

"You don't just walk away. I went out the same way I went in. Beat down."

And right then, something told me that was where he got the scar on his lip. Intuition or a hunch, it didn't matter. I stepped over to him and traced the faint line with my finger. His lips were soft. The scar smooth. He took my hand in his, and stared down at my fingers.

"Ended up in the hospital. I'm cool with Las Cobras. Grew up with most of the guys. But it's not the same with any of them anymore. They knew Pedro and me were like brothers. Losing him affected me the most." He paused. "I wish I would have been with him that night. Maybe things would have been different."

I knew what he meant. In the face of losing someone, the ones left behind often played the what-if game. What if I hadn't made my dad promise to take me out on the boat that day?

Anthony's hand moved to my face.

My arms slid over his shoulders.

We stared into each other's eyes. His were serious. Sad. Full of grief. Maybe mine reflected the same emotions. For the first time I wondered if we were destined to meet. To comfort each other's pain when we hadn't gotten the comfort we needed from those closest to us.

He walked me backward toward the bed. Slowly, we slid down. My chest tingled. He shifted next to me, looking down at me, brushing hair away from my neck with his fingertips.

My pulse fluttering with anticipation, he leaned down and pressed his lips to mine.

23. Connected

My cheeks were flushed, my body hot. Mouth tender. The soft sounds of kisses filled my head.

Anthony was above me, his hand under my shirt. His hips against mine. My arms were around him, fingers sliding through his hair as he kissed me long and deep. Every touch felt good. Sensitive. I wanted to kiss him forever.

A loud knock sounded at his door. "Anthony, open up."

My eyes widened. I pulled back. *"Is your dad home?"* I whispered. I couldn't picture the demanding voice coming from his grandfather.

Anthony muttered, "Shit." Then louder, "Be out in a minute."

In a frantic rush, I pushed him away and pulled my shirt down, trying awkwardly to adjust my bra. *Oh damn. Oh damn.*

"It's all right. Just my brother. Dad's out of the picture. Mom works late."

I nodded, but now my cheeks were flushed with embarrassment. I stood, blowing out a breath. He had a small mirror on his wall. My cheeks were definitely red, my lips pinker than normal. No doubt anyone would know what we'd been doing. I ran my fingers through my hair. Serious bed head.

Anthony came up behind me and pulled me back against him. His skin was hot and he smelled really good. He kissed my neck. "I left a mark."

I pulled my shirt away from my neck. A hickey the size of my thumbnail was on my collarbone. Something else to hide from Mom.

"You okay?"

I nodded with a forced smile. I was definitely okay. It was just awkward to be caught like this. So dang awkward.

He met my eyes in the mirror. "Don't be embarrassed, okay?"

A smile spread across my mouth as I squeezed my eyes shut. "Sure."

"Kara."

I opened my eyes.

"You're wonderful."

I flicked my eyes down, caught off guard. I wanted to protest, but pleasure stirred inside my chest. I knew guys said pretty words to get girls to go further with them, but Anthony's compliment didn't feel like that.

Anthony took my hand and I followed him to the door.

"What do you want, Carlos?"

A guy a head shorter than Anthony leaned against the wall beside the doorway. His face was round, his eyebrows the same shape as Anthony's. A tattoo was etched on his neck. He grinned when he saw us. A silver cap covered his incisor tooth. "Didn't know you had . . . company, bro."

Meeting his gaze, I was sucked into some strange inferno where everything surrounding me intensified.

His soft laugh echoed in my ears. The television sounds from the front room shifted low and deep. The hairs on my arms stood straight up. The pounding of my heartbeats stretched thin. My breathing slowed. The hallway faded away.

Dark brown eyes.

His white T-shirt flashed bright. His skin was brown. A faint mustache grew above his top lip. His black hair was shaved so close to his head I could see his scalp.

My eyes slid down his neck, past the collar of his shirt. Lower . . .

The image formed.

Carlos in the night. His eyes wide, frantic, sweat on his forehead.

"Damn. What'd you do to her, bro?"

"Kara. *Kara.*"

I blinked at Anthony. His hand was on my shoulder. "I'm okay. Sorry."

He bent his knees a little so that we were eye level. "Are you all right? What happened?"

"I think, ah, I just need something to drink." I wet my dry lips.

"Go get her a Coke," Anthony tossed over his shoulder to Carlos.

Anthony straightened, put his hands on each side of my neck, and tilted my chin up with his thumbs. "What's wrong?"

I pulled away. "Nothing." Guilt sliced into me for the lie, because yeah, there was something wrong. Something that involved his brother. But how could I tell him? He wouldn't understand and I didn't understand what the sign meant.

I rubbed at my earlobe. Was Carlos connected to my latest puzzle? Was something going to happen to him at night?

Carlos strolled back with a soda. I took the cold can in my hand. "Thanks."

"No problem. Eh, I was going to ask if you wanted to kick it at Julio's, but . . . I see you're busy."

Anthony nodded. "I'll come by later."

"Cool. Lates."

Carlos walked backward out of the room, looking me up and down, then turned away. I stared at his back. His pants sagged low on his butt, and he walked with a slow gait, like he had all the time in the world to get where he was going. I frowned.

"Kara."

"Um." I continued to rub at the small loop in my ear. "I need to get to work." I picked up my tote bag.

Anthony still stood by the door. He slipped his hands inside his jean pockets. He had bed head too, but his looked good on him. He was watching me. Too closely.

"Why do I get the feeling you have more secrets?"

I stilled. "I don't know."

He came closer and placed a hand on my shoulder. "You can tell me."

I wouldn't meet his gaze. I stared at the tiny lines in the fabric of his tank top. "Tell you what?"

"Anything you need to."

Our arms went around each other for a hug and I held on tight, closing my eyes.

The truth was, I couldn't.

Not everything.

24. Always A Fighter

Near the end of my shift that evening, I went to throw out two bags of trash into the Dumpster. Holding my breath, I heaved the bulging black bags over the edge of the large tub. The smell was always disgusting.

A small rock skidding against the ground made me turn.

My hand went to my chest.

The Feather Man stood in front of me about three feet away, mumbling under his breath.

I tried to go around him, and he turned with me. One arm like a thin, gnarled tree branch stretched out in front of him. His shoulders were covered with a navy blue blazer. The top pocket was partly torn from the threads. Two collared shirts underneath. His hair was long and wavy. His skin was brown and marked with lines. Bloodshot eyes stared wide, as if he saw something I couldn't.

My heart beat fast. I just needed to make it to the back door.

"El padre."

I shook my head. "I don't understand. *No entiendo.*"

He took a step, grabbed my arm with tight, thin fingers. *"El hombre es bueno."* His lips pulled back with the pronunciation of each word, revealing yellowish teeth.

My face flashed hot, then cold. I wrenched my arm away and ran to the back door, slamming it closed behind me. I stood there a moment, chest heaving. My whole body felt like it had been dipped in a pool of trepidation, and all the traces were dripping off of me as I tried to calm down.

I knew what the Feather Man had said: *The man is good.*

I just didn't understand what he meant. The Feather Man wasn't exactly all there in his mind. I believed he was homeless, but I wasn't sure. He often mumbled to himself things I didn't understand. Normally I would have brushed an encounter like this off, but I knew what I felt with the Feather Man the first time we'd crossed paths.

A sign that never formed on him. Just like with Anthony.

Several years had passed since my first encounter with the Feather Man. I was thirteen and had just started to solve simple puzzles . . .

I walked beside Mom, with Jason trailing behind, as we strolled Valdez's Old Town. The shops were small and unique, and Mom enjoyed browsing and stopping for lunch at one of the bistros. Jason hadn't wanted to tag along, but Mom had made him, and he in turn made his annoyance clear by listening to his headphones the entire time and playing mute.

"Oh, look at that! There's a sale at my favorite antique shop. I wonder if that clock is marked down." Mom tapped a finger to her mouth. "It's pretty packed. I'll just slip in real quick to check. Be right back."

Jason had already sat down on a brick bench with his back to me. I figured he didn't want my company. I took a few steps to the next window's shop. I noticed a man with a cowboy hat with several feathers stuck out of the band, cleaning the windows from inside the store. He sprayed from a bottle, then streaked the glass with a small windshield wiper.

I watched his lazy strokes, and as he pulled the wiper down in front of me, I blinked.

Soft footsteps clicked loud on pavement. The muted chatter of voices from inside the store echoed in my mind. A blackbird squawked above me. Each flicker of my pulse stretched and lengthened like melted taffy. The store shifted to a dull background while the man exploded with color. The feathers in his hat glinted like sparkles. Black, white, yellow, gray, brown.

Black eyes.

Each line on his brown face became more distinct. His black hair, peppered with silver, touched his shoulders and covered the lower half of his face.

My eyes slid down his sharp nose, past his beard, past the buttons of his collared shirt, and the lapels of his navy blue jacket. Lower . . . to his chest.

I frowned, took a step closer to the window.

No flickering, no image.

No sign.

Nothing.

"Of course, the clock I wanted wasn't marked down."

I sucked in air. I'd been holding my breath.

Mom pulled me to face her, her fingers digging into my forearm. "What is it? Kara? Are you okay?" Her green eyes were wide, frightened. Jason stood beside her, studying me with the same look of fear.

They were afraid I was seeing things again. That the time in Jameson hadn't worked. Hadn't cured me. I could read the mirrored horror on their faces. If I wasn't cured, life would be awful again. It would remind them of the accident. It would remind them of Dad.

My hands fisted at my sides as I forced a smile. "Fine. I'm fine. Isn't that the cutest handmade purse in there?"

They both glanced inside the store. A purse made out of magazine clippings was propped on a table behind the Feather Man.

Mom smiled and nodded, her shoulders sagging with relief. "Yes, it is. Adorable." Her laugh was sharp. "Well, I'm starved. Let's go eat."

Blinking away the memory, I pushed off the door of the

pizzeria. That had been the first time I'd covered up seeing a sign in front of my family.

Rubbing the chill off my arms, I went back to work. The Feather Man meant something . . . but what? And to who? And still the question plagued me, were Anthony and the Feather Man connected in some way?

Tonight I was off at seven. I was usually heading home at six on Sundays, but my manager asked me to stay one more hour when someone called in sick. So it was a shock when I saw Freddie Howards come through the door . . .

. . . with my brother.

Jason's brows pulled together when he nodded his head at me.

I lifted my hand in a hesitant wave.

Freddie and my brother are friends.

That information alone sent a shiver running down my back. With Freddie being part of the gun puzzle, I didn't need Jason anywhere near him.

They went over to the pool table. I joined them touching the silver loop in my right ear.

"Hey," I said.

"Thought you'd be off already," Jason said.

Freddie smiled at me. "How's it going?"

"You know Kara?" Jason asked him.

He flashed a grin. No matter how buzzed he'd been, he must have remembered me from the party. He slid an arm around my shoulders. "You can say that."

Heat crawled up my neck.

Jason's frown deepened. "What the hell does that mean?"

"I didn't know you guys were friends," I said.

"Since VH basketball. I played JV," Freddie said.

Jason had played basketball his junior and senior year. I hadn't known Freddie had played during his sophomore year before he became the star of the football team.

"I'm off in fifteen." I cleared my throat. "You want to order?"

Freddie said, "We're waiting for someone." He lifted his eyebrows. "Want to join us?"

"No, she doesn't," Jason interrupted. "Do you need a ride?"

I tugged at my apron. "No."

"Who's picking you up?" By the way he jerked up his chin, with attitude and suspicion, I knew he already guessed the answer.

The loud rumble of Anthony's car drew our attention through the windows toward the parking lot. The headlights flashed off. I immediately shifted away from Freddie. His arm slid off, but I knew it was too late. Anthony could see everything.

"You're not leaving with him."

Jason's superior tone irritated me. He was becoming more like Mom all the time. "Jason, stop trying to run my life."

"I'm not. I'm looking out for you."

I glanced out at Anthony. *Please, don't come in.* "I'm going to clock out. Just don't start anything, Jason."

I hurried to clock out my time card and get my bag. When I came out, Jason and Freddie were playing pool. Jason bent over the table with his cue, but they were both deliberately staring out the window. Anthony leaned against the hood of the car, arms crossed, looking straight ahead.

The back of my neck tingled.

Even with the tension, I couldn't just leave without saying good-bye. I walked over to Jason. "See you later." I wanted to tell him not to tell Mom about Anthony, but it was a lost cause. He already had. He would again.

My gut twisted at the thought. *What would Mom do when she found out I didn't listen to her about seeing Anthony?*

Jason looked at me, pressed a finger to the mark on my neck. His expression was serious. "You don't know what you're getting yourself into, Kara."

I shook my head. I was tired of people telling me that. *Maybe, but I know what feels right.*

Freddie came up and slid his arm around me again. A nervous flutter hit my gut as I stepped away.

Too late.

Anthony strode inside, gripped Freddie's jacket, and shoved him against the pool table. Freddie grabbed Anthony back, but Anthony clearly had the advantage as he pushed Freddie down on the table.

Balls clanked and scattered. A pool cue crashed to the floor. A customer let out a startled screech.

My stomach pitched.

"Keep your hands off of her." Anthony's voice was low and totally pissed.

"Anthony, let's just go." I reached for him.

Jason yanked me away by my arm. "Stay out of it, Kara."

"Hey! Break it up!" My manager, Tom, appeared and pulled Anthony off of Freddie.

Anthony jerked away from Tom, hands up. His chest rose up and down.

Freddie straightened, shooting Anthony a fierce glare. His face flushed with anger. "We'll finish this, homeboy."

"Anytime," Anthony said.

"All of you out," Tom demanded. "Now."

I swallowed hard. I couldn't bring myself to say anything to Tom.

Anthony looked at me and offered his hand. He was still breathing hard. His eyebrows pressed low over his eyes.

I pulled away from Jason and gripped Anthony's hand in return.

We rushed out and got into Anthony's Chevelle. He drove out of the lot, burning tires. The rear end slid a little on the asphalt.

The night cloaked us. The silence between us was thick and uncomfortable. I didn't know what to say. I didn't know what he was thinking. I watched the bright streetlights fly by. Anthony finally pulled into a diner parking lot and cut the engine.

"I'm sorry," Anthony said, voice quiet. He wouldn't look at me.

I blinked. Shouldn't I be apologizing for my brother and Freddie? "What for?"

"I'm not sorry for pulling that fu—" He stopped short, gripped his steering wheel with one hand. "For getting him off of you. I'm sorry if I scared you. Don't be scared of me, Kara."

I released my seat belt and scooted closer, leaning over the gearshift, placing my hand on his chin so he would look at me. "I know you wouldn't lay your hands on me like that."

"I wouldn't. It's just . . ." He turned to look away again. "I'm a fighter, Kara. Always have been." *Always will* was left unsaid. "It was one of the reasons I joined up with the Cobras. Something inside me always wanted to fight when I was younger. Always pissed about something. Then just when I think I've wised up, something triggers it." He lifted a fist to his chest. "This anger."

In his way, Anthony was asking me to accept who he was. I understood that. I only wished I could do the same.

"I'm not asking you to be someone you're not," I whispered. Nudging his face to me again, I closed my eyes and brushed my lips against his.

Kissing Anthony was natural now. My pulse flickered, my body relaxed. I knew how his body felt pressed against mine. How he held my face, or moved his fingers down my neck. How he smelled . . . how he tasted.

Anthony was an outsider in my life, like I was in his. Both of us imperfect. Real. With past regrets. And we accepted that about each other.

He pulled back, rested his forehead against mine. Our noses brushed. "You mean a lot to me, Kara."

And he meant a lot to me. I just couldn't say it back. Even though I was being more honest with Anthony than I'd been with anyone in a long time, there was still so much I kept hidden from him. It wasn't just the signs and how I followed them that bothered me. That was like a survivor's instinct, to keep that part of me secret.

But I wondered . . . if keeping secret the sign I'd seen on his brother was doing more harm than good.

Gun
F.H. (Arguing with someone to meet after school.)
F.H. (Gun aimed at him at Dishes by cops.)
Dom. (Gun fired two shots.)

Carlos
(In the night . . .)

Anthony
(A sign that never appeared on him.)
(Knows Dom.)
(C.G. is his brother.)
(Confrontation with F.H.)

In the quiet of my room, I stared at Anthony's card. I couldn't ignore that even though I wasn't seeing signs on him, he was connected to the puzzle in more ways than one. It was almost like he was a center of a wheel, and all the clues were the spokes that connected to him in one way or another.

I just didn't know why.

Tired, but not willing to let my brain settle, I logged onto my blog.

My eyes widened, and goose bumps rose along my arms. I had fifteen comments on my latest blog entry.

A couple of spammers. The rest anonymous, giving me advice or their thoughts about my ability. Nothing cryptic, just honesty.

tarabear said . . .

i saw a ghost once when i was five years old. no one believes me till this day!! but I know what i saw, so just know there are people out in blogland who understand. maybe not totally understand but are rooting for you!!

anonymous said . . .

i've never seen a ghost but i really believe there's life after death. and well, this gift of yours has to come from a higher power or something. anyway, it totally rocks, and I love your blog.

"Crazy," I whispered.

No one had to know about the smile teasing my mouth.

SECRET FATES:
The Sign Seer's Blog

This puzzle is becoming more personal, and truthfully, I'm afraid. I try to tell myself not to be scared. I feel like I've been running from scared for the past six years, and it's still catching up to me.

I saw another image. On my boyfriend's brother.

There is no way I can tell my boyfriend that I'm worried about his brother . . . and I don't even know how I could, even if I had the guts. Not without him looking at me like something is wrong with me. Not without losing him. And not when I don't even know what the sign means.

He's really special to me. No other boy has treated me as if he cared about me before. But if I don't try to tell him, his brother could be in danger. And he's already lost someone very close to him. I don't want to see that happen again.

If I look at the bigger picture, my boyfriend seems to be a main connection that intersects between multiple signs.

Am I too involved with him to see this puzzle objectively? Is the answer right in front of my face?

I'm just not sure what to do . . .

—Sign Seer

25. Anonymous

"**H**ey."

I didn't really sneak up on Danielle in front of our school locker, but she flinched anyway.

Her back was to me, her hand in her bag. "Shit, you scared me."

"I'd say sorry, but . . ."

She turned, smiling. She looked a little tired. "But, you're not."

I attempted an eyebrow wiggle.

She pushed her curls over her shoulder. "Before I forget, I'm leaving school early today."

"Why, what's up?"

She shrugged. "My mom called. A friend of the family died."

Immediately Dad flashed into my mind. *I hear about death, I think of Dad. It's like a trigger.* "That's awful . . . I'm sorry. What happened?"

"Motorcycle accident. Mom and Dad are all upset." She went quiet for a moment. I thought she was going to say more, but instead she sort of zoned out on me, going quiet and staring at the floor.

I played with my earring. "Were you close?"

She blinked. "What?"

"Did you know the friend well?"

"Oh. No. He's, um, actually been in a coma for a couple of weeks. We just got word he passed, and now we have to go back to our hometown for, you know, the funeral and stuff."

Yeah, I knew about funerals. The strange thing was I could barely remember my father's. At that time in my life all there had been was pain and sadness, and not just my own. Mom's, Jason's, aunts, uncles, cousins, friends. *It's like you suffocate from everyone's unbearable sorrow until that's all you remember.*

"So I'll see you in a couple of days," she said.

"Okay. Tell your family I'm sorry."

"Yeah, will do."

I reached out to her, but found myself hesitating. I wanted to hug her, let her know I was there for her even though I couldn't bring myself to say so. She walked away and the moment was gone.

I turned to trade my binder for a notebook. A magazine clipping stuck out between my books. With a sense of sudden dread, I pulled out the clipping. It was a computer advertisement for iMac.

In black lettering across the screen was:

Sign Seer

My stomach flipped. My palms dampened. No. *No.*
Someone knows.

I leaned against a locker. A sudden flash appeared behind my eyes. People whispered behind their hands, pointing at me, laughing. Looking at me like I was some kind of freak because of the weird, unnatural things I shared on my blog.

Prickles danced across my face.

Just one whisper to one kid could start the rumors of Crazy Kara all over again. And I'd be back there, alone, medicated by Dr. Hathaway, trying to convince everyone I was sane. The memory came back instantly . . .

"I'm just telling you the medication is too strong for me," I said quietly to the nurse. The tiny cup of meds was in my hand. I still felt a little off from yesterday's meds. The idea of adding more made my stomach quiver.

"You'll need to take it up with your doctor."

The problem was, I was so out of it by the time I met with the doctor I could barely concentrate. "Please, can I call my mother?"

"Not until visiting hour. Go on now," she said, holding a small cup with water.

Defeated, I tipped the cup into my mouth, then the water, swallowed twice.

"Open."

I opened my mouth, shifted my tongue. No more pills.

Crossing my arms, I walked back toward my room. The walls were peach, reminding me of the time I was sick on peach sherbet ice cream and splashed it all over my bed. I thought about sticking my finger down my throat and gagging up the pills, but I hated throwing up. And they'd know. They knew everything in Jameson.

I had to convince them I was okay. I had to get out of here.

I passed girls my age chatting, a couple playing board games. Didn't they hate being here? Why did they act as if nothing was wrong?

In my room a half an hour later, I felt the meds spreading through my blood. My mind went foggy. My tongue was dry and thick. My shoulders slumped, and I just wanted to lie down in bed. For a little while . . .

"Let's go, Kara. Group time." The nurse again.

So tired. But I had to go, had to cooperate. I sat up in bed. My entire body was heavy and light at the same time. Using the wall, I pushed myself up.

One step, and then I was sprawled on the cold floor.

"Come on, Kara. You have to want to get out of bed. You have to want to get better."

I felt the first hint of anger. I wasn't sick. I didn't want to be here. *And I'd be able to walk if you didn't drug me!*

Swallowing back tears, I pushed myself to my knees. Then my feet.

Using the bed, I stood.

Then I walked carefully to the group area to pretend I was the happiest girl on earth.

"Hey, Kara!"

I actually jumped before I shifted toward the voice in the school hallway.

Mindy Tall approached me, ponytail bouncing, braces beaming. She was the girl that was into as many school clubs and activities as she could handle. It's not like we were friends, we'd just had a couple of classes together, but you didn't have to be pals with Mindy Tall. She wasn't afraid to talk to anybody.

"Hey, are you okay? Do you need a nurse or something?"

I shook my head, swallowed. "I'm . . . good."

She looked at me like she wasn't sure if she should believe me. "Uh, okay. I just wanted to know if you got that pic I slipped in your locker?"

The photo of Danielle and me in the lunch line. "You. You put that in my locker?"

"Yeah, through the vent. I was in a rush and had an extra copy from yearbook. Sorry, I didn't slip it in with a note."

"Um, that's fine. Thanks." I folded the note in my hand. "Have you slipped anything else in since then?"

"Nope. Oh, there's Bobby Germaine. Hey, Bobby!" She took off down the hall, flagging down her next priority.

I watched her as I tore the note in half, then again, tearing it to pieces. I turned, made sure I was steady on my feet, and shut my locker. As I passed a garbage can, I sprinkled the pieces across the inside of the can.

I tried my best to shake the feeling of someone knowing about the blog, someone watching my every move without me knowing who or why. But the lurking sensation was there like a ghost I couldn't see.

After school, I took public transpo home. I leaned my tired head against the cool glass of the window. *I'm going to have to delete the blog.* I had to. Couldn't risk anyone knowing it was me behind Secret Fates. Each time the bus stopped, the glass made my head vibrate. The bus drove past the lot of the news station where Jason's pickup was parked. On a whim, when the driver stopped a block away, I got off.

I walked quickly, looking over my shoulder. A weird feeling rushed through me. Like I was being watched. Like something was closing in. I rubbed the back of my neck as if I could rub away the sensation.

Entering the building, I told the receptionist behind the glass that I was there to see my brother. She mentioned he'd just walked by to go on break and pointed down a hallway.

I signed in and went down the hall, gripping the straps of my school bag. I spotted Jason right away just outside a door and started toward him.

"This is bullshit," Jason said into his cell phone, his hand resting on the crown of his head. "I don't care, don't you get it?"

I hesitated. Who could he be talking to? The almost desperate tone of his voice told me he wasn't talking to Mom. I had an urge to just sneak back the way I came.

He shifted on his feet, and his eyes locked with mine. His hand dropped from his head. "Look, I gotta go. Just trust me, okay?"

He flipped his phone shut, and slipped it into his front pocket. Then nodded his head to me, moving his bangs out of his eyes at the same time. "We keep running into each other. Something wrong?"

Where to start? "Do you have a few minutes to talk?"

"Barely. Let's walk." I followed him to an employee break room. A few people lounged at the tables. Jason went over to a rotating food machine and started putting in coins.

"So what's up?" he asked.

"Well . . ." I swallowed. "I wanted to know what your problem is with Anthony?"

He didn't glance at me as he chose a sandwich, but he did sigh like the issue with Anthony was the farthest thing from his mind and he just didn't want to deal with it. "He's bad news. Attitude. Got gang ties."

"How do you know?"

He made a point of looking me in the eye. "I played basketball against his school, Kara. My junior year he was with his gang, starting trouble with my team. He and his friends were thrown out of the auditorium. I remember him because he made a stupid scene. He's a loser."

I almost didn't believe it, but I'd known Anthony had

been with the Cobras before his best friend died. It could be true. "He's changed, Jason—"

He let out a harsh sound. "Kara, you're smarter than this."

Heat rushed to my cheeks. I grabbed at the first thing that popped into my head. "Well, what about Freddie?"

Jason snorted. "What about him?"

"He's the one who looks for trouble anywhere he can. *You* shouldn't be hanging out with *him*."

"Kara . . ." he said with a frustrated growl.

Irritated, I shot out, "Since when have you even cared who I hang out with, anyway?"

"Lower your voice, damn it." He grabbed his sandwich and looked at me. I thought he'd meet my attitude head-on with his own, but his expression revealed something else.

Uncertainty?

"I know I haven't been . . ." He leaned closer. "I know I suck as a brother, all right? I wasn't there for you after Dad. I let Mom put you through all that."

Sighing, I said, "You were a kid. Mom wouldn't have listened." *You hadn't even listened to me.*

"I don't know. Sometimes I think if I had done things different, things would have been different. Maybe if I'd gone with you guys that day."

My gut tightened. "No."

"Maybe I could have helped."

"Maybe *you* would have just been hurt."

I'd been the one seeing the doctors, but what about my brother? He hadn't talked to anyone about his grief. And no one had thought to ask because all the attention was on me. Realizing this was like having another block removed from my wall of control, leaving me unsteady. Unsure.

"Maybe," he said. "That day Dad talked to me."

It was a habit between us to always say "That day" if we ever had to talk about the accident. It's not like there was another day that had shaken our family to the core.

I stepped closer for even the smallest piece of Dad. "What did he say?"

"We'd been in a dumb argument, you and me. I don't even remember what it was about anymore. All I remember is Dad sitting me down, telling me how I was the older brother. How, as I got older, I'd learn to look after you. I was still all pissed, so I didn't go with you guys on the boat."

"Jason—"

"I haven't been looking out for you like Dad wanted." He looked at me so intensely I wanted to reach out and hold him. "What does that say about me, Kara?" He closed his eyes a moment. "I have to get back to work."

"Wait."

He turned and walked away. I tightened my arms around myself as I watched him go. Walking in here, I'd wanted something to be settled between us, and all I'd done was dig up more pain.

I was beginning to think nothing could ever be settled.

And that being a broken family forever was our future.

At home, I logged onto my blog. Someone knew it was me.

But how could they know? I'd been *so* careful. I shifted in my desk chair. On my iMac, I navigated to my user page, scrolled the mouse over the delete button, and clicked.

Warning: Are you sure you want to delete your blog forever?

I shut my eyes. I'd been getting nearly a hundred hits a day and more comments. People actually asking me questions about what I could see, how it felt. Some flaming stuff too, letting me know I was a nutcase.

I'd been expecting that kind of feedback. But I'd also gotten comments from people who believed me. Here on the Net, I wasn't so alone. Here, I was free.

How could I lose all that? How could I just let it go on a couple of cryptic notes?

My knee bouncing, I clicked "cancel" to the warning. Maybe the note writer didn't really know it was me and was trying to scare me into outing myself. I clicked over to my main blog page.

At the bottom of the latest entry "anonymous" left a single-word comment this time:

anonymous said . . .
friend

I could feel the tension in my shoulders as I checked the stats up to the time of posting and printed out the ISP address. Too bad I wasn't some cyber geek who could actually track ISPs to a location. I went back to all the anonymous entries that were suspicious and printed the stats out. I took a highlighter and marked each entry that could be the same person and compared the addresses.

I blew out a frustrated breath.

The ISPs were all different. Either different people were posting these odd anonymous comments or they were protecting themselves with proxies or different servers.

I didn't know who anonymous was, or the note writer, but I wouldn't let them stop me from blogging. Not yet, anyway.

26. The Race

I didn't mention to my mom that Danielle was out of town for the funeral of a family friend. Danielle and extra shifts at the pizzeria were my only alibis for being with Anthony. Luckily, Mrs. Salazar and my mom had never gone further than polite hellos, so they didn't communicate to confirm any of our plans. They trusted us, since we never gave them reasons not to.

I loved being with Anthony. We shared things with each other that we'd never shared with anyone before. Little things we hadn't thought anyone would have cared about. We laughed at each other's teasing. We touched when we didn't have to. His hand on my knee, a finger stroke down my neck. My fingers on his wrist. My hand on his shoulder. Sometimes he'd just drive and we'd sit, content, listening to the music that boomed from his speakers, watching town life go by.

Being with Anthony was like eating a twisted piece of a two-flavored candy. I got two satisfactions in one sweet bite. I couldn't deny how the signs seemed to appear more frequently when I was with him. Seeing more signs moved me closer to the solution to the puzzle, and that meant relief from the headaches and, more important, that soon I'd try my best to help someone from an unfortunate fate.

After we caught a movie Friday night, Anthony pulled into the lot of a liquor store called Zipper's. It was still a little overwhelming riding in Anthony's Chevelle. The sound of the engine drew attention, which was surreal since I tried my best to cruise under everyone's radar.

"Who are all these people?" A cluster of cars were parked in the lot. Kids leaning against cars—probably fast cars. Vintage like Anthony's, some newer street racers I'd seen around town that made a *zooooom* sound as they drove.

"Locals who like it fast," he said.

Low music sounded from multiple cars, and everyone stared as Anthony slid into a slot, cutting the engine.

Wait, the music hadn't been on low, it was Anthony's engine that had muffled the sound of everything else.

"What up, dawg?" Some skinny guy in a gray beanie smacked palms with Anthony through his open window. "You looking to ride?"

Anthony nodded once. "Thinking about it."

"Cool. I'll let you know."

"What's he talking about?" I murmured to Anthony as the beanie guy sauntered to the next car window.

"Wants to know if I want to race."

"Do you?"

"Depends."

I lifted my eyebrows. "On what?"

"If anybody's willing."

I didn't respond.

He reached over and put his hand on my thigh. "Want to get out?"

I looked around. Saw only strangers. "Maybe in a few minutes."

"I'll be back." He got out, shut his door, and leaned back against his car.

I took out my Rubik's Cube from my bag. I twisted and turned, not particularly caring if I matched colors. I liked that Anthony brought me along, but I just wasn't comfortable with the street racing. It was dangerous, and danger could turn deadly before you knew it.

Anthony was talking to someone again. Maybe the beanie guy. Maybe someone else. I zoned them out and focused on the twisting of the cube. Anthony shifted. I glanced in his direction—

The sounds rushed upon me like a tidal wave. Music, engines revving, chatter—spiking at different volumes.

Yo, man, it's cool . . . His engine's hot . . . That chump's going down . . .

A guy stood beside Anthony. My chest squeezed as Anthony faded to gray, and the kid brightened. His hands were tucked inside the front of a sweatshirt that glowed a vivid apple green. An image shimmered together.

A red vehicle—some kind of vintage pickup—driving fast. Headlights flashing. Tires burning.

The pickup swerving out of control.

I blinked and the kid shifted sideways, colors flashing back to normal.

"Boo!" a voice shouted into my window.

I jumped in my seat, making an embarrassing girl squeak. My heart pounded.

Carlos let out an annoying laugh next to me. His hand covered his mouth as he leaned the other hand on the open window of my door.

"Damn, girl, I got you *good*."

I forced a smile, trying to settle my nerves. "Yeah. Guess you did."

He moved away, shoulders still quivering, as he rounded the hood to his brother. Rolling my eyes, I shoved my cube into my tote. Annoyance and apprehension struggled inside me.

Moments later, Anthony opened the door and slid in. "No one's up to racing me tonight. They know what I got and don't want to eat my exhaust."

He smiled at his own teasing, but I couldn't bring myself to return the gesture. The muscles in my shoulders were stiff with tension.

"So I guess that means someone else is going to race," I said.

"Yeah, guy named Pyro I was talking to right now and another kid, Montez. Both got fast rides. Sorry about Carlos. He's got a warped sense of humor."

"He can't race tonight," I said quietly.

Anthony frowned. "Who? Carlos?"

I swallowed. "Could you take me to Pyro's car?"

He continued to look at me. He was waiting for me to explain. I wasn't planning to.

"Please," I added.

Anthony's frown didn't clear as he got out of the car, but he didn't ask questions as we walked to Pyro's ride. The vehicle was a red vintage truck with faded purple flames on the fenders. The same pickup I'd seen flash on Pyro.

Anthony nodded his head toward the truck. "El Camino, '72. Know the guy who did the ghost flames. Sweet job."

I grabbed his wrist. "How can we get him not to race?"

Anthony chuckled. "The deal's set. Not much going to change that."

"Maybe . . ." I wet my lips. "You'll race the other guy instead."

Anthony pulled his arm away, tucked his hands inside his jean pockets, and tilted his head. "I got the vibe you didn't want me to."

He was right. The thought of Anthony racing made me nervous. But I hadn't seen Anthony's Chevelle losing control.

I kicked a small rock in the parking lot, watching it skitter across the cement to land against a tire. "I don't think Pyro should race."

"Why?"

I shook my head, tightened my fists inside the pockets of my jacket. "You won't understand."

He stared at me for a long moment, long enough for my shoulders to tighten.

What am I doing? Am I saying too much?

"I'll see what I can do." Anthony walked off. I went back to his car and slid into the passenger seat, cradling my head into my hands. "Idiot," I whispered.

Anthony probably thought I was a total nut job.

By the time I had called myself twenty different kinds of idiot, he finally returned, sliding into the driver's seat. His expression was unreadable.

He started the car.

I rubbed my hands on my thighs. "So . . ."

"So. We race."

Old Miner's Road was a two-lane long back road that went on for miles. Lights were few and far between. The sides of the road were wire fenced with a few secluded homes like mere shadows in the overcast of night. Other kids had followed and parked along the side road, leaving headlights on. Music still bumped and boomed.

Anthony shut off the car.

"Anthony."

He looked at me, his expression relaxed. Or was he just not interested?

I wanted to say I was sorry. He didn't know he was stopping someone from having an accident or worse. He didn't know I was trying to help someone but had no control over the situation, and was using him because I knew that he did.

"Please, be careful."

His mouth curved. "Always." He nodded with his chin toward the door. "You're going to have to get out."

"Oh, okay."

"Don't take it the wrong way. Girlfriends just don't ride along." The sides of his mouth tilted up. "It's like a rule."

I lifted my eyebrows. "What about that day on the street with the Mustang?"

"That was different. I was just messing around. This is the real deal. And it's safer by myself."

My neck tingled. "Maybe this is a bad idea." Maybe fate would play a twisted game, and if Pyro's pickup was out of the race, someone else's car would lose control. A small voice told me I was just being paranoid, but I couldn't help the doubts from forming. When the signs showed me the clues of someone's fate, they didn't jump to someone else. I knew that.

I *did*.

"Can't back out now. Relax. It's a straight shot, a quarter mile." He leaned forward and gave me a quick kiss on the lips. "Now out," he said without heat.

Without thinking, I reached into my bag and pulled out my cube. "Here."

He took the puzzle, his eyebrows lifting.

"Brings me luck." Sliding my hand behind his warm neck, I gave him a real kiss, deep, meaningful, and fast, before pulling back.

His eyes remained closed a few seconds longer. "Maybe I should race more often."

I smiled and pushed open the heavy door. "Let's take it one race at a time."

He set the Rubik's Cube on a small tray below his CD player and started the car.

I crossed to the far side of the road as Anthony pulled his car up next to another. His opponent's car was a blue vintage Camaro, and the engine's volume thrummed against Anthony's.

Anthony's wheels spun against the asphalt, tires burning, a puff of heated smoke releasing into the air.

Carlos stepped beside me, his arm brushing mine. "So now you're trying to tell my brother what to do."

I took a step away and glanced at him. His eyes were lazy, his mouth set in a flat line. He rubbed his nose and sniffed.

"I don't tell Anthony what to do."

I watched Anthony pull on a black fitted beanie over his head, the top resting just over his eyes. He slid on fingerless gloves.

"Not what I hear," Carlos spat out. His eyes were no longer lazy, but narrowed. "First he says his girl don't want him to race, then he goes back and says he's in. You trying to make him look like a punk?"

I shook my head, wide-eyed. *"No."* Yeah, I was a serious idiot.

Carlos bumped me with his shoulder hard enough for me to step back. My gut twisted. He moved in front of my face. Too close.

"Don't be coming to our neighborhood, looking to slum with my bro, *chica.*"

I stepped back again. "I'm not—"

He only moved closer. "You walk around with your nose up in the air. Don't talk to no one. Think your mutt ass is all better than us."

I swallowed past the sudden thickening in my throat. "That's not true."

"All I'm saying is you better not mess with my brother's head, then walk away. When he's done with you, fine, but not until then."

He stepped away just as Anthony punched the gas and sped off.

27. Denial

"It's Garcia, dude! Garcia beat Montez's ass!" a voice rang out on someone's speakerphone. Hoots and whistles shot out from the waiting group.

My hands clapped together. "Thank you," I whispered. Relief was warm and wonderful in my chest as I waited for Anthony to return. I was glad he'd won, but I was *thrilled* he was safe.

Anthony drove back to the starting line, the engine of his Chevelle vibrating with victory. Kids crowded around his car as he pulled off his beanie and gloves.

I stayed back on the side of the road, eyeing Carlos with caution. He pushed his way to his brother and opened the car door. The brothers grabbed hands, slid fingers, and knocked fists. A serious bond there. I wouldn't be the one to cause problems between them. Carlos's attitude toward me would have to stay between Carlos and me, and I would definitely steer clear of him from now on.

Anthony must have asked his brother something because Carlos nodded his head toward me, and Anthony looked in my direction.

I smiled as he walked over.

He took my hand in his. "Your good luck charm worked."

"That was the plan."

In a sudden move he wrapped his arms around my waist, lifted me off my feet, and kissed me—fast and quick. "Let me get paid and we're outta here."

I laughed. "Okay."

He set me to my feet and his opponent tossed him a wad of cash. We got in his car and drove down the dark road. Anthony blasted the music, his fingers tapping the steering wheel. If excitement could give off electricity, he'd be sizzling in his seat.

I grinned in his direction.

Anthony glanced over, lowered the music. "What is it?"

I pointed a finger at him. "You are so pumped."

He smiled. "Hell *yeah*. My blood's humming. I can feel it. Going fast like that, it's a rush I can't explain."

"Dangerous and a little scary, I think." Before he could comment, I spotted a vehicle on the side of the road. "Look."

"It's Pyro." Anthony pulled alongside the El Camino. Pyro and a friend were checking under the hood.

Pyro walked to Anthony's window. "Dude, steering went out."

Even with all that energy that had been coursing through Anthony, I could swear he'd gone suddenly still. He didn't look over at me, and he was quiet. Then he said, "What happened?"

Pyro shook his head. "I was driving out and just lost control. Power steering gearbox must've gone out. Don't know. Fuck, man, it's a good thing I didn't race tonight."

"Yeah. I'll give you guys a lift."

After the guys hopped in the back, I settled back in my seat. Another unfortunate fate stopped. Made good. I didn't speak as we drove to Pyro's house. Pyro and his friend filled my silence with talk about the race.

I kept my gaze pointed forward and wondered what was running through Anthony's head. Was he suspicious about how I knew not to let Pyro race? Or would he think it all a coincidence?

We said our good-byes to the guys at Pyro's house, and Anthony blasted the radio on the way to mine. He parked a block away. I think he believed I asked him to do that because his car was so loud, but the truth was I was keeping him a secret from my mom.

He turned off the car, and I unbuckled my seat belt.

Before I could say anything—about the race, about Pyro, about what had happened to his pickup—Anthony leaned toward me and kissed me. Not soft, but fast.

I put my arms around him and he pulled me to him so that I sat on his lap, legs over his gearshift. His arms held me against him.

He kissed my face, my neck, my ear. Soft brushes that made me shiver.

The air was cold outside, but inside the car was warm.

My breathing increased, and my body seemed to tighten. Everywhere he touched tingled. I ran my hands down his shoulders, to feel his body. Lean. Strong.

I could smell him, that distinct scent that was him. Being this close to him made my chest squeeze.

I never felt this way about anyone before.

I couldn't imagine feeling this way about anyone else ever again.

We kissed as the windows fogged, and the moonlight shined down on us.

And I knew.

I loved him.

"We better stop," Anthony said near my ear.

I nodded, trying to calm my pulse.

Sometimes I didn't want to stop. I wanted to keep kissing him, but I knew that could lead to deeper things I had yet to experience. That I wasn't sure I was ready for.

He settled me against his chest, his arms around me. He cracked the windows to let cool air in. His head leaning back against his seat. Our heartbeats were both moving fast. My legs were still draped over the stick shift.

He grabbed my Rubik's Cube and handed it to me. "Thanks again for the good luck charm."

I smiled. "You're welcome." I started turning the rows.

"You ever solve it?"

"I'm on fifty-eight."

"What? Days?"

"I've solved the cube fifty-eight times."

He chuckled quietly. "Damn."

"Well, that's over six years. Plus there's a certain method to solve the puzzle no matter how the squares are aligned. I try not to use it. It's pretty ingrained, though. I just like puzzles."

"Me too . . . sometimes." He didn't say much after that.

"So, how much did you win tonight?"

"Three."

My eyebrows lifted. "As in hundred?"

"Yeah, the price varies. I don't throw in more than five."

"Wow."

I felt him shrug against me. "Goes to the car. Saving up."

"Yeah, for what?"

He shook his head. "Nothing, it's dumb."

I shifted back so I could see him in the dark. My interest was piqued. "Tell me, please. I really want to know."

He sighed. "One day, I want to open my own garage. Maybe. I've always been good with cars." He smiled. "It's all I'm good at. I work side jobs and Marco, my boss, he talks about a partnership all the time. I'm not a team player. Don't know the first thing about running a business. Just want to work on cars, and at the same time, be my own man."

I was quiet because I was surprised. But why should I have been? Just because I had no idea what my future held didn't mean Anthony was the same way.

"Told you it's stupid."

"No, it's not. I think it's really great. It's just, I don't even know how to look that far ahead. It's great that you do."

"Why don't you?"

Because you never knew when things would change. When one wrong move could throw you off course and change a life forever. I traced a finger along the scar on his lip. Maybe it was the dark of night, the newfound feelings I had for him. But I took a risk, my stomach tingling.

"Do you believe in fate?" I asked him.

A few beats passed and I almost regretted asking when he said, "Not sure. Sometimes I do and sometimes I think we make our own."

I licked my lips. "I think there's fate, and that sometimes it can be changed."

He shook his head. "How?"

"Maybe . . . if someone saw what the future could bring." I still wondered why Anthony didn't question me about how I knew Pyro shouldn't race. Or even just mention how it was weird, or a good thing that I asked Anthony to race in his place. It was like he completely ignored the possibility of what could have happened.

Another long silence fell on us.

"What, like, a psychic?" He laughed a little and shifted. Almost as if he was pulling away from me, not only physically but emotionally.

"Something like that . . . you really don't believe in it? What about hunches and intuition if something doesn't feel right—"

He shifted abruptly again, and I sat up. "Look, it's not my thing, all right?" His tone stung with irritation.

"Okay." I moved back over to my seat. The loss of his warmth made me shiver. I shoved my cube into my tote. The tingling had moved from my stomach straight to my chest.

I crossed my arms and rubbed the heel of my hand against the uncomfortable feeling. I'd thought if anyone would be open-minded about my ability, it would be Anthony. Why did the people I care about never want to take the time to believe me?

I guess I felt a little betrayed with the way he was acting. We'd connected with so many different things, and now he was all bent out of shape over me asking him a few questions. It made me want to make him feel uncomfortable.

"So what about the party?" I asked, my voice hoarse.

From the corner of my vision, I saw him glance at me. "What?"

I stared straight ahead at the foggy windshield. It was surreal that just moments ago, we'd misted these windows with our heavy breathing. "If we hadn't run into each other, would you have called me?"

"Yeah."

"If you hadn't seen Freddie in my face, would you even have cared enough to ask me to be your girlfriend?"

"Kara—"

I grabbed my bag, pulled the handle, and shoved open the door. *Just forget it.*

"Kara, come on." He reached for me, but being small had

advantages; I slipped through his fingers. I stepped out onto the sidewalk. I heard him get out on his side. I opened the heavy car door too wide. The bottom scraped along the sidewalk and wouldn't budge.

"Shit." Annoyance and guilt warred inside me because I got the door stuck. He was rounding the hood, so I just ran to get away from him.

"Damn it, Kara!"

I thought I had the advantage if he stopped to fix his door, but before I could get across one home's large front grass, he hooked his arm around my waist and we fell on the grass. I sucked in a breath. He shifted so that I fell on him, grunted, then he rolled to pin me under him.

I shoved at him. It was like trying to push solid rock. "Get. Off. Of Me."

"Kara, stop. Just listen."

"No." I kept struggling, knowing it was a lost cause. I was used to leaving things unfinished. I felt like my life was one big unsolved puzzle and there was never anyone else to try to figure it out. I didn't talk things through with anyone. I disagreed with my mother until the last word was given, and then we both ran off. Deep inside a voice told me I was doing the same thing with Anthony. I just couldn't get past my hurt feelings to want to change it.

He grabbed my wrists and shifted them to either side of me, then leaned down to kiss me.

I turned my head so that he got my cheek. He brushed his lips there, then down my neck, then to my ear.

He spoke softly. "I didn't mean to hurt you when I didn't call. I couldn't stop thinking about you, and damn, Kara, I got scared, all right? I didn't know if I wanted someone serious in my life. It wasn't you. It was me. I swear you were on my mind all the time. Even in my dreams."

I stopped struggling.

"I'm sorry," he murmured.

I turned my head, but I wouldn't meet his eyes.

"I am, Kara."

A sigh escaped my lips. "I'm sorry too." And I was, for trying to push something on him that he didn't believe in. Accepting who we were was what made us work. I couldn't blame him for not being open to the secret demons that drove me, for being normal and regular. Maybe that was part of his appeal, and one of the reasons I wanted to be with him. Because I did want to be like everyone else.

But I wasn't. I never would be. Any more than I'd ever be able to share my secret with him.

28. Forbidden Feelings

"Let me walk you to your house."

"No, it's okay. It's just a few houses down."

"Kara, it's dark. If you won't let me drive you to your house, I'm walking you."

Anthony's protective ways were nice at times, but it was irritatingly inconvenient when I was trying to hide him from my mother. That uncomfortable feeling from our argument still stretched between us like a bubble. It felt fragile, like one false move could make it pop.

How could I even have thought to bring up the idea of changing fate to him?

"Fine," I said. "But just a little ways. I told you my mom is weird about me dating." That was all I could think to tell him. It seemed too hurtful to tell the truth, that my mom was prejudiced against who he was as a person.

We held hands. The cold air was like a soft caress against my flushed cheeks, hopefully covering any signs of our make-out session.

"Here's good." I stopped him two houses down.

He leaned down and kissed me softly on the mouth. "What time do you work tomorrow?"

"Two to six."

"I can give you a ride home."

"Okay, but I really have to go." I turned and jogged to my door, my tote knocking against my hip. I unlocked the door and stepped into the warmth of the house, hoping Mom was already in her room.

I flashed on her face in my mind and knew she probably wasn't in bed. I was about to run up the stairs when I saw her standing at the landing. I gripped the banister. My damp palms slid against the wood.

"Hi," I said.

"Your mascara is smeared under your eyes."

I raised my fingers to my face. "Oh—"

"I know you're still seeing him, Kara."

Dread settled at the bottom of my gut. I crossed my arms against my chest. We both knew who she was talking about.

"After I told you not to associate with him anymore."

"I can't just turn off my feelings because you say so." My voice was quiet, nearly as devoid of emotion as her tone.

"Feelings? You're a kid, Kara. You think you know about real feelings?"

Anger filled me like coffee poured to the brim of a cup. My arms fell at my sides, my bag falling to the floor.

"Yes, I do! That's what you don't understand. I can feel anger, and pain, and sadness." *Suffocation.* "I may be just a kid to you, but I *feel.* And *yes,* I care about him."

"Oh for crying out loud."

"Not that you'd understand, but he treats me well. And you can't take that away."

"How can a gang member be so wonderful? Did you know he's been arrested twice? Spent time in juvenile detention?"

My eyes widened. "You—you had him looked into?" *Did she forget about my own sordid past?*

"Someone at the office did me a favor. I do what I have to. Just like now. You're grounded until I say otherwise."

Tears sprang into my eyes. "Why? What have I done that's so wrong?" *Why do you keep doing this to me?*

"I told you already. I told you *not* to see him, and you went ahead anyway."

"I don't understand how you think you can control every part of my life! My job, seeing Dr. Hathaway, and now who I date? Don't you see what you're doing?"

In a small part of my head, I knew I was crossing the line, showing too much emotion. Disagreeing with my mother was okay to a certain extent, but shouting back only showed her I was out of control. And what she might do in response could be really scary. But everyone has a limit and I had reached mine.

"I'm trying to keep you safe."

"Safe? No, Mom! You're pushing me away just like you did Jason! Just like you've taken bits and pieces of Dad away."

Her eyes widened. *"What?"*

A lump lodged in my throat. "I just can't take it anymore!" I ran up the stairs, shoved past her to my room, and slammed the door, locking it.

Tears streamed down my cheeks as I fell onto my bed. I grabbed my pillow and held on as so much pain fought inside of me. God, it felt like it was tearing me apart.

I wanted to pound my fists against something. I wanted to scream at the top of my lungs. I couldn't. It wasn't allowed.

"*Daddy*," I whispered, "*help me.*"

"Mom, why won't you believe me? I saw them. I saw people walk through walls. I wasn't dreaming."

"Kara, calm down. Just relax." Mom pushed the button to call for the nurse.

I shook my head. "You're not listening to me. *Please*, just listen to me. Why would I make something like this up?"

The nurse walked into the room. She had a syringe in her hand. "Let's take it easy, Kara." She walked to my IV. She stuck the tip of the needle into the thin tube that led to the back of my hand.

I ripped the IV from the needle taped to the back of my

hand. "No! No more drugs." Whatever was in that syringe made me sleep. I didn't want to sleep.

"Kara, please," Mom pleaded with me. She started to hold me down. "You can't lose control like this."

I struggled against her. "Stop!"

Suddenly the nurse was grabbing at me too. Holding me down. Then someone else. I screamed, and I fought. Not because I was mad. I fought out of fear.

Five days later, after my father's funeral, I was taken to Jameson.

29. Another Excuse

I called in sick to work on Saturday. I sent Anthony a text message pretty much saying the same and turned off my phone. I felt so low, like nothing could pick me up. I pulled myself out of bed to pretend to eat what my mom put in front of me.

A peanut butter sandwich on whole wheat bread, a scoop of plain Lay's, and a glass of cranberry juice.

She still treated me like a baby. She'd been making the same lunch for me ever since I was little. When would things change? When would she finally see me as seventeen? And not the little girl who she believed was crazy?

Probably never . . .

We sat in silence as I picked at my sandwich and ate a few chips. When I finally pushed myself away from the table and headed up the stairs, I heard her pick up the phone and dial.

"Hi, Dr. Hathaway, this is Katherine Martinez. If you could give me a call back when you have a free moment, I'd appreciate it." She paused. "I think we ought to discuss more about Jameson."

My stomach squeezed. I jogged to my room, grabbed my Rubik's Cube, and sat on the edge of my bed. My heart beat fast. My fingers trembled. It felt like the chips and juice I'd eaten would come right back up.

I shut my eyes for a moment. *It's okay. Everything will be okay.*

Left row forward. Right row back.

For years, I'd tried to show my mom what she wanted to see. I hid my ability from everyone.

Turn cube over. Turn middle row.

I hardly argued with her even when everything inside me screamed in protest. I went to the stupid sessions with Dr. Hathaway, even though I knew they wouldn't work for me.

White square to white square.

I showed her a side of me that wasn't really *me,* all in the hope she would finally label me normal.

And I'd done it all in fear. Fear of what she held over me.

I gripped the cube with all my strength.

It had all been for nothing.

SECRET FATES:
The Sign Seer's Blog

Have you ever felt that no matter how hard you try to do something, it just never turns out the way you want it? That it's out of your hands. Completely.

That's how I feel right now. That everything is out of my hands. Yeah, I follow signs. I try to help others from facing unfortunate fates, but I can't do anything about my own. I feel like I'm riding passenger in a reckless car at high speed about to slam into a brick wall, and there's nothing I can do except brace myself for the impact.

It's so frustrating!

It's become clear that no matter what I do, it doesn't change what is bound to happen to me. I'm done trying to stop whatever my future might hold. I'm done pretending I live a perfect life, that I'm happy, and that everything is just as it should be.

I'm done pretending to be someone that's not really me.

—Sign Seer

30. Discovered

"Kara, let's get going," Mom called from downstairs. "I don't want to keep Dr. Hathaway waiting."

Yeah, wouldn't want that. I swiped some lipstick across my mouth, folded my lips against each other, and grabbed my pack before heading down.

Mom heard me and grabbed her briefcase and keys. She opened the garage door from the kitchen and glanced at me. Then did a double take.

I fiddled with the loop in my ear.

Her eyes went from the black Vans that covered my feet to the black socks, the fitted black Dickies pants, and the black ribbed tank top. Strands of my hair were weaved in several small braids. And of course, there was the makeup. The usual mascara, plus the black eyeliner and the maroon lipstick I'd snagged from her makeup collection.

It wasn't like I'd dyed my hair pink and tattooed my body, but it was a drastic change in my mother's eyes. I hadn't worn all black in front of her ever since she started complaining about it when I started high school.

It was my way of saying that I was tired of trying to be the girl she wanted, when it didn't stop her from siccing Dr. Hathaway on me and thinking about sending me away again.

I walked past her into the garage. "I'll be in the car."

"We've had a setback, Kara." Dr. Hathaway actually tsked in disapproval.

I lifted my chin. "I don't feel we have." My arms were crossed as I leaned back defiantly on the paisley couch.

"This drastic change? It's a message to us, isn't it, Kara? To your mother? To me? You're trying to tell us about your unhappiness."

I shifted uneasily on the couch. "I'm trying to be who I am and not someone else's image of me."

"Your mother's? Your father's image of you?"

"Stop talking about him like you know him," I snapped. I looked away from her and swallowed hard. I wanted to run out the door and scream at the top of my lungs.

"I think it's time for a prescription."

My stomach tightened. "No, I don't need anything."

"It's just to relax you—"

"I'm fine."

"It'll help you to rest at night. Something mild. I'll give it to your mother."

Go ahead. I wasn't going to take any pills.

Never again.

Two hours later, my shoulder bumped someone in the hallway at VHS. A kid gave me a dirty look, then a quick once-over of my face. He'd likely seen me around school before, looking ordinary. Without much makeup. Plain. Unnoticeable.

"Sorry," I muttered, and kept walking toward my locker. I ran my hand across my forehead. A headache throbbed along my skull.

Mom had cut off my caffeine intake over the weekend and hadn't left me alone long enough to brew my own stash of coffee. It had been another struggle to hide my emotions with Dr. Hathaway during our morning session. After she wrote the prescription she continued on about my "latest altercation," and "deliberate disobeying of your mother's requests." And of course, my recent "lack of appetite," and she just couldn't get over this morning's "drastic change."

It had only given Dr. Hathaway more fuel against me. But I realized that nothing would keep them from waiting for me to drop the ball.

I spotted Danielle at our locker. She was back in town. She glanced over her shoulder in the direction opposite me and slipped a folded piece of paper from her back pocket inside the locker. She shut the door before jogging off.

She was gone before I could stop her. I spun the combo, unlocked the locker, and started trading books. Danielle's folded paper had familiar thick black marker on it.

The back of my neck tingled.

Swallowing hard, I opened the paper to see a screen shot of my blog. My fingers began to tremble as I turned over the paper to read:

I Know Who You Are

My gaze flew down the hall, trying to spot Danielle. I couldn't see her. I wasn't sure I wanted to. The bell rang. A few kids rushed past me. I held the picture to my chest, leaned against the lockers, and slid down to the floor.

"I know who you are too."

I'd been getting text messages from Anthony that morning. If the "WTF?"s were any indication of his attitude, I wasn't sure I wanted to talk to him. He'd left one voice mail on Sunday: "Call me." I hadn't turned on my cell until after my session with Dr. Hathaway.

I took a bathroom pass during fourth period before lunch. The scent of bathroom sewer always grossed me out. Two girls were at the sink, doing their hair and whispering to each other. I turned my back to them and dialed Anthony's cell.

"Hi," I said.

Silence, then, "What's going on, Kara? Why are you avoiding me?"

"It's not you. I'm having some trouble. I'm grounded."

I could hear him let out a breath. "Sounds like we both had great weekends. What happened?"

"It's . . . a long story."

"When can I see you?"

"I don't know." Everything was getting to me. And now this thing with Danielle, her knowing about my ability, and sending me these creepy, cryptic notes. I'd taken two aspirin, but my head continued to pound.

"I just don't know what to do," I said, my voice cracking. I peeked back at the girls. They stared at me as they walked out.

"Hey, take it easy. Where are you?"

"School."

"I'm picking you up." His voice was determined.

I shook my head even though he couldn't see. "Can't. I have to stay. You have work."

"I'm off today. I'll pick you up for lunch. What time's your break?"

I told him before I could talk myself out of it. I didn't know how I would face Danielle at lunch, pretending I didn't know it was her leaving the notes. I mean if she knew everything—about my blog, my secrets—why didn't she just tell me?

Everything felt so out of control. More than just a jumbled puzzle. More like various puzzles thrown together with pieces that would never fit. I hadn't felt like this since the day when I first entered Jameson Hospital. Nearly six years ago . . .

*   *   *

"I packed the bag myself," Mom told the attendant as he searched my suitcase. Her arms were crossed as she glanced at me.

I sat on a chair, my hair tied back, my hands stuffed in my sweatshirt pockets. I knew what was happening, but my mind was foggy with medication. My emotions trapped under a cloud I couldn't break.

Don't leave me here, I whispered in my mind.

"It's procedure, Mrs. Martinez. We can't have any contraband, nothing brought in that could be harmful to one of our girls." She removed my belt, toenail clippers, and shoelaces from one pair of shoes.

I shifted my eyes to the attendant and blinked.

A ringing telephone echoed against my eardrums. Murmuring voices heightened in volume.

Thank you for calling . . . Do you have the chart on . . . The grounds are beautiful . . .

The hairs on my arms stood up. My heartbeats increased. My breathing slowed. Everything surrounding the woman flicked to light gray images.

She has blue eyes.

The green of her sweater pulsed. Her skin gleamed like porcelain. Her red hair nearly blinded me.

My eyes moved down her throat even as my pulse flickered rapidly and my breaths went too fast.

The image was a women's mountain bicycle, dented and lying on the ground, one wheel spinning.

I blinked and my mother was on her knees in front of me, tears in her eyes. "Kara. Help her, she's hyperventilating!"

"Kara, can you hear me?" The woman was beside my mother, checking my pulse, then my eyes. "I need you to calm down, Kara. Can you do that for me?"

I shut my eyes and everything went black.

31. Different Inside

Anthony slid his sunglasses down his nose as I got into the car. "You . . . okay?" He seemed pretty interested in my fitted pants and tank.

I was about to answer "Fine" when I decided to be truthful. "Actually, I don't know."

"You look really good, but a little different. You did something more with your makeup. Hair." He nodded. "Nice."

"Thanks, I feel different."

He drove the car. "What do you want to eat?"

"I'm not hungry, but I could really use some coffee." I got a text message from Danielle. She wanted to know where I was for lunch. Should I text her? Should I tell her that I know it's been her leaving the notes? I turned my phone off instead.

Anthony drove me to a drive-through Starbucks and ordered me a Grande Caffé Mocha.

I sighed as I drank the hot, sweet coffee. "You said something about us both having great weekends on the phone. Did something happen?"

"Just with my brother. He's going through some stuff. Personal. Doing crazy shit." He shook his head. "Don't know how to help him through it."

"I'm sorry." I really meant it. Families were hard. "Maybe I can help in some way."

"Thanks, but it's a brother thing. We'll handle it. What happened with you and your mom?"

I stared down at the cover of my coffee and wiped off a drop of light brown liquid. "I don't really feel like talking about it either . . . sorry."

His lips curved up. "It's cool. I'll just keep driving."

He drove to the West Side, pointing out things he used to do growing up. The movie theater he would sneak into with Pedro. The elementary school where he first kissed a girl. The store he shoplifted candy from until he got caught and smacked by the store owner. The park where he used to ride his bike and play basketball.

Whether it was his intention or not, he showed me that the West Side wasn't all about danger. That violence was just one facet of the neighborhoods here. Families just like mine lived here, and had their ups and downs like everybody else. It was too bad I couldn't convince my mother of this.

But then I couldn't convince her of a lot of things.

"Let's stop here," I said.

Anthony pulled along the sidewalk. The park was old with rusted monkey bars, two swings, and a wooden and steel play set with a slide. A little boy played on the bars while his *abuelita* sat on a bench.

I walked onto the sand and sat on the swing. The toes of my shoes drew lines in the sand. Anthony followed and grabbed the chains on either side of me.

"Talk to me, Kara," he said, looking down at me.

"What do you want to talk about?"

"There's something different about you. Not just your look, but something inside."

I stared out into the street, watching cars drive by. "I'm tired of being someone I'm not. I'm tired of being afraid."

"You're one of the bravest girls I know."

His words made me hesitate. I shook my head. "You sound like you don't know me all that well."

"Look at me." When I did, he said, "If you're not brave, who was the girl who was about to run back into Dishes with a rumble going on to look for her friend? Who was the girl who risked herself by saving that little *niña* from falling down a hole?

"You, Kara Martinez."

But he didn't know everything. Didn't know I was still afraid of my past and secrets. Afraid of not following the signs. I was afraid of the day he might look at me like he never truly knew me.

My eyes stung. "What about the beach? I can't even set

foot on it without flipping out. I can't even stand up to my mom about why she's totally closed off everything that reminds me of my father."

I couldn't stop her from sending me away, and I was too scared to try.

"You will. One day, you will."

I shook my head. "Can I ask you something else?"

"Go ahead."

"If one day I was taken away . . . would you wait for me to come back?"

Concern moved across his face. "Where are you going?"

"Just tell me, please. I need to know, without telling you anything else."

"No."

I swallowed and blinked back tears.

"I'd go after you," he said.

32. Notes

Anthony dropped me off at the end of fifth period. I made it just in time for sixth. After class, I walked slowly to my locker.

Danielle was already there waiting. She didn't smile, or give her signature lift of the eyebrows. If I hadn't been watching her so closely I probably wouldn't have noticed the dark circles under her eyes, or that her cheeks seemed thinner.

I stopped in front of her. We didn't speak at first, and we seemed to be looking everywhere but at each other. The rush of kids filled the awkward silence.

Finally Danielle shifted against the locker. "So, where were you at lunch?"

"With Anthony."

She nodded, then looked away. "Could have dropped a text."

I opened my tote and took out the folded paper. I held it out to her.

She looked at the paper, but didn't move to take it.

"Here, just open it."

She took the paper and unfolded it. "Kara . . ."

I pushed a braid behind my ear. "I saw you put it in the locker this morning."

She stared at the blog printout. "I can explain."

"So you know, then."

"I'm not sure what I know," she said quietly.

"Why have you been putting these notes in the locker, Danielle? What did you hope to make me feel? Scared? Hurt?"

She met my eyes. "I didn't—"

"Because it hurt me to find out it's been you."

"It wasn't to hurt you."

"What does that even mean?"

"Okay, just listen. It'll sound weird, but I'd signed up for a blog account. I never had the guts to post anything on it. I often check the site out and read the most recent updated blogs. Secret Fates popped up. I started reading, and I couldn't believe how much it sounded like you. I've been reading your essays for two years, Kara, and I couldn't help thinking it was you. The death of your father. Your cat. But I wasn't sure. After you found the photo of us in the locker, I got the idea of leaving you notes. I know it was wrong, but I was shocked by the blog. I thought maybe you'd share the notes with me, then I'd be able to tell if it was just all in my head. But you didn't."

"You could have just asked if it was me." Even as the

words left my mouth, I knew she'd never have done that. Not when it was something she believed was too personal.

"How could I, Kara? We don't go there. We just don't."

My throat thickened because she was right. We'd had a surface friendship since the beginning, full of jokes, gossip, and hanging out. Surface. Never anything more important or meaningful. I'd known this for two years, accepted it, but now the way our friendship worked finally bothered me.

It finally hurt.

At the moment, I couldn't agree with her or let her off the hook. I nudged her aside to get my stuff. I just wanted to get out of there.

"Kara, I wouldn't intentionally try and hurt or scare you. I just didn't know how to bring it up to you. I mean, the signs. That's—"

I glanced at her. "What? Crazy?"

She didn't answer, but it was plain on her face.

I shut the locker. "Yeah, you not hurting me? That's what I used to think."

Danielle shook her head and walked away. She kept her head down. Guilt nearly had me calling her back just so everything would go back to the way it had been before she left for the funeral.

But if I knew anything, it was that I couldn't turn back time.

And maybe I didn't want to go back to normal anymore.

Anthony did me the favor of driving me to an authentic Mexican market on the West Side. I picked up a pint of *carne asada,* corn tortillas, fresh guacamole, and refried beans and rice. He couldn't stand that he was missing out and bought a burrito with everything.

I tried calling Jason to come and eat at home. He said he was working late, had stuff to do. Maybe he did, but I also knew he was avoiding home. I didn't blame him. If I'd had a choice, I wouldn't be there either.

I set all the food on the kitchen table along with two place settings, then sat and waited. I pictured the three of us sitting there a few years before. Mom and Jason actually having a decent conversation, about basketball, about school, with me listening. I saw Mom smile, brush her hair away from her face. Saw Jason almost laugh. He'd been about fifteen. And then the memory was gone.

The only sounds were the kitchen clock on the wall ticking with each passing second, and the refrigerator humming on and off. I could smell the grilled meat, and my stomach growled.

Still I waited.

I wanted to take another stand. I wanted to finally know if my theories about Mom avoiding a part of our heritage were right all along.

I wanted her to know that even though she tried her best to ignore who we were, she wouldn't win.

And damn, I wanted her to admit it.

Mom finally came through the door with her briefcase and an armful of files. A strand of hair had fallen out of her

French twist and brushed her pale cheek. Her lipstick was worn off. She turned toward the kitchen table and glanced at me, then at all the food.

"What are you doing?"

"I got dinner tonight." I started making my tacos. Spooning beans, meat, and guacamole onto a tortilla. I wouldn't meet her eyes. She just stood there watching me. My stomach twisted, and I hoped I'd be able to enjoy the food.

"You know you're grounded, Kara Marie."

"It was a quick trip on the way home."

More silence.

Is she going to stand there all night?

"You better clean all this up," she said, her voice flat. "I have work to do." She walked out of the kitchen and took her work upstairs, not even bothering to check the mail on the counter.

I stared at my full plate and the bowls of food before me.

A headache started to throb in the back of my head. I shoved my plate away, propped my elbows on the table, and rested my head in my hands.

I wasn't so hungry anymore.

SECRET FATES:
The Sign Seer's Blog

Days are stretching by slowly. I have yet to solve the long, on-going "gun" puzzle. To say I've had personal distractions would be an understatement. And I know that's partly why it's taken me this long.

If I could put off solving the puzzle until life was smoother, I would. But the headaches are gaining in strength the longer I'm sitting back doing nothing, and that tells me I'm running out of time.

It's gotten to the point where aspirin isn't helping, and I may go insane with pain. This is one of those times when loneliness sets in. When I wish I had someone who understands what I'm going through. Someone who could help me decide what to do next.

That's why I'm so grateful for this blog, for those of you who read and leave your comments of encouragement. When I started this blog, I hadn't thought about what the positive feedback could mean to me. Truthfully, I hadn't thought there would be any.

And now that I'm feeling so alone, it's a connection I've grown to value.

As for the puzzle, all I know is that I'm going to have to make a move soon. Or I could very well fail. And if someone gets hurt because of me . . . I just don't know how I'll be able to handle it.

But you'll be the first to know.

—Sign Seer

33. Revealed

Anthony: u sure u want to go?
Me: yes. :) be here @ 11.
Anthony: ok. cant wait to kiss u.

I stood in front of my brother's old bedroom window. Jason had snuck out a lot during his high school years and miraculously Mom never discovered his absence. But then she'd always been focused on me. Tonight I didn't care. With my grounding and Anthony's work schedule, we hadn't seen each other since the day he picked me up from school, nearly a week ago.

I hadn't spoken to Danielle since then, either . . .

The headaches were increasingly painful, and I was becoming snappier with Mom. She watched me closely anytime we were in the same room. I felt like popping my eyes open wide and staring right back at her, just so she knew how irritating she was being.

On a recent phone conversation with the couch doctor, Jameson was mentioned again. It made chills run down my back. I was beginning to feel as if Monday would be it. I would go to my regular appointment with Dr. Hathaway and be shipped off.

I envisioned myself fighting against orderlies, trying to take me away.

First of all, I wasn't a fighter anymore, so that would never happen. Second, I would probably go meekly like a lost kitten. *Damn, I don't want to go.*

Anthony had mentioned a party on the West Side, and I had jumped at the chance. Whether I was grounded or on my way to Jameson, I had to make a move on the puzzle, and the party was my only chance.

Felt like my last chance.

I slid the window open, praying it wouldn't squeak. Jason had always kept the window nice and lubricated for silence. I licked my lips and looked at the tree. *That's a seriously far reach for the tree branch from the window.*

I stepped up onto the windowsill and stretched my left arm and leg out onto the branch. The wood was sturdy and rough beneath my fingers. The cold air made me shiver. I took a breath and just sort of leaped and managed to hang by both hands, and lifted my legs to wrap around the rough branch.

Breathing with exertion—I so needed more exercise—I stretched over with one arm and slid the window mostly closed.

A twig crunched below me.

I froze.

"It's me. Let go. I'll catch you."

Relief sunk through my body. I shut my eyes, dropped my legs, and held on by my hands for just a second before I lost my grip.

Yikes. I fell onto Anthony and we collapsed onto the wet grass.

Anthony made an *umph* sound.

I'd jarred my ankle when I landed, and I just held on to him tight, shaking silently with laughter. For some reason, I'd always laughed when I was in physical pain, even as tears built in my eyes. My left cheek rubbed against the softness of his flannel jacket, my hands gripping his shoulders. My heart ached with missing him. I raised my head and scooted so that I aligned our faces.

His eyes smiled into mine. "You all right?"

I kissed him.

His arms wrapped around me, kissing me back.

"I missed you," he whispered as our lips parted for one quick moment.

I smiled against his mouth and mumbled, "Same here."

He gave me one more kiss. "Let's get going."

We stood, wiping the wetness off our hands onto our jeans. I rotated my ankle to shake off the mild ache. Anthony pulled two leaves from my hair. Lacing our chilled fingers, we jogged away into the night.

The party was in a newer housing section built within the last five years. You could easily jump onto the highway and head out of town. Cars were parked all along the street and music could be heard from outside.

I slipped my phone out of my pocket and turned it off, leaving it in Anthony's car. Unease was heavy in my mind. If Mom found me gone, there'd be hell to pay. But I was tired of it all, Dr. Hathaway, walking on a careful edge with both her and Mom, never knowing when either might pull the rug out from under me and turn my life upside down. I had an entire six months before I was eighteen, but I'd been beginning to wonder if I'd ever make it without ending up trapped in Jameson.

"So you want a beer?" Anthony asked.

"Sure, I'll take a cup."

Linking our fingers, I followed him to the keg. Josie was leaning against a wall with her boyfriend. She gave me a dirty look. My first instinct was to turn away. Yeah, she intimidated me with her street-tough attitude. She was a fighter and I wasn't. She was a real Latina, and according to her and Carlos that made me less than them.

I wasn't less, just like they weren't less than me. No matter what side of town we lived on, and how diluted my blood. I held her gaze as we walked by. Anthony nodded his head toward her, and she did the same, then looked away. I couldn't say it meant anything, but no matter how small the victory, I was glad I hadn't broken eye contact first.

We walked into the kitchen. It was spacious, but the dense crowd seemed to fill almost every inch. The line was long and seemed to be moving at a snail's pace.

"This could take a while," Anthony said.

"We could skip the beer."

"May have to."

Someone moved through the crowd, shouting, "Move the fuck out of the way."

I was bumped against Anthony. He caught me against him. "You okay?"

"Yeah."

Anthony nodded with his head to someone behind me. "Yo, Carlos! Chill out, bro."

I turned, expecting to see Anthony's brother.

Instead, my view collided with Dominique's profile. Carlos was in her face. She shook her head and turned toward me.

The music roared around me, the hairs on my arms standing. Voices smeared together. Murmurs. Whispers. Laughter.

I'm so wasted . . . Did you get her number . . . Just get her high first . . .

The people in the room flashed to gray, as if each of them held a light within them and one by one they clicked off. And Dominique glowed.

Her eyes glimmered brown.

Black hair waved over her shoulders. The black of her shirt gleamed like silk, and in the center . . .

A baby slept on the center of her chest.

The signs shifted in my mind, like a kaleidoscope of visions. Gun. Freddie. Carlos. Dominique. It had been Carlos who I'd seen fighting with Freddie at Dishes. His walk had been familiar to me and I hadn't been able to place him before. Freddie and Carlos were fighting over Dominique . . . and she was pregnant.

"Kara . . ."

I had to talk to Dominique. Needed to warn her. Carlos might do something stupid. She . . . and the baby were in danger.

I scanned the kitchen. They'd both disappeared.

A sharp pain arrowed into my scalp. I winced, lifting a hand to my head.

"Kara, what's wrong?" Anthony was watching me closely.

I rubbed my temple. "Dominique."

"Talk to me, Kara, what's going on?"

"Does Carlos have some kind of nickname?"

"Yeah, Chico, since we were little . . . why?"

She's having a great time without Chico.

"Is he part of the Cobras?"

"What? Why does it matter?"

"Just tell me."

"No, he's not, all right? He hangs with them. They're our boys."

"He was there that night, at Dishes. Fighting with Freddie."

He blew out a frustrated breath. "I know, Kara. I helped get him the hell out of there."

A crash came from the front room. Then screams.

Someone shouted, "Fight!"

Anthony slid his arm around my waist. "Shit," he murmured. "Stay close." Bodies pushed us toward the front room. I was smashed against Anthony.

"Watch the fuck out," Anthony yelled at someone. "What'd you say?"

"Anthony, it's okay. Let's just get out of here."

"Asshole," he muttered under his breath.

The fight had escalated into a rumble. A fistful of guys fought, smashing into furniture and a couple of unlucky kids not quick enough to get out of the way.

People rushed around. Some drank beer and watched. I thought we'd be heading out, but Anthony glided me to a clear space near the opening of a hallway.

"Fuck, it's Carlos." Anthony shoved a hand through his hair. He vibrated with tension beside me.

Pedro whispered in my mind.

Anthony had to be thinking of Pedro and of the deadly outcome when he hadn't been there for his best friend. Now something could happen to Carlos. At the same time I could tell he was also worried about me getting hurt if he left me alone.

I touched his shoulder. "Anthony, go get him. I'm going to stay right here and wait for you."

He shook his head.

"Help him. He needs you. I'll be fine. Hurry."

He held on to my shoulders and met my gaze. "Promise you'll stay right here?"

I took his right hand from my shoulder, and like he had with me in his bedroom the day I told him about losing my dad, I gripped his hand with a reassuring squeeze. "Yes."

He nodded once, muttered "All right" under his breath, and lunged into the fight, reaching for his brother. Someone grabbed him by his flannel and shoved him away. Anthony whirled and threw his fist against the guy.

Freddie.

Shit.

I fought the urge to run out there and drag Anthony away. But I knew I'd probably just be thrown around like a rag doll. I grabbed my cube from my tote and, with my back against the wall, sank down to the carpeted floor.

Turn first row forward. Bottom row back.

Freddie flashed into my mind with the first sign. Gun.

Dominique. The gun firing two shots.

Carlos in the night, scared.

The baby.

Freddie. Dominique.

Carlos had fought Freddie at Dishes.

Freddie flirting with me.

Jennifer's voice: *As far as I know, he doesn't. Rob is always bragging how they play the field, and not just football.*

Something still didn't seem right. Freddie and Dominique. Why did they not feel right?

Again, the sharp pain dug inside my head. I leaned my head against the wall and shut my eyes.

Someone flashed in mind, and I didn't understand. Didn't *want* to understand.

A door swung open in front of me. I glanced up . . .

. . . and blinked. "No."

34. Gunpoint

The person who'd flashed in my mind stood in front of me.

"What are you doing here?" Jason snapped.

His arm was around Dominique. She looked at me, then at my brother.

I stood, shaking my head in denial of what was right in front of my face. I'd never seen signs on anyone in my family, and here was the truth. My brother was the one who'd been involved with Dominique. Not Freddie. The first sign had likely flashed on Freddie because he'd been the closest connection to my brother. It had been Jason all along.

The hickey on his neck.

The phone call I'd overheard at the news station.

Freddie and Jason, waiting to meet someone.

Gun. This was a gun puzzle.

My pulse spiked. I had to get him out of here.

Anthony yelled for me. I couldn't see him anymore, and he couldn't see me.

I turned toward the front room but Jason grabbed my arm. "Kara, what are you doing?"

I yanked my arm free. "Anthony's out there with Freddie. Look, you need to leave the party."

"Let them settle their problem, Kara."

Frustration flashed hot inside of me. "What problem, Jason? That Anthony used to be part of a gang? Or do you mean the problem of Freddie starting trouble with him?"

Jason swore under his breath. "Both of you wait here. I'll see what's happening." Jason pushed through the crowd.

"No, wait—" *It's not safe for you. Carlos is out there.* But he'd already moved out of earshot.

Anxiety swam through my blood. It took everything not to run out and try to bring Anthony and Jason back to safety myself. But it wasn't just Jason who might be in danger.

I stuffed my cube in my tote and looked at Dominique. "How long have you been seeing my brother?"

She pushed her hair over her shoulder. "About three months."

"Have you been . . . seeing Carlos and Jason at the same time?"

Her eyes narrowed. "No. I'm not that much of a bitch. After I broke up with Carlos, I met Jason. Carlos won't accept that it's over."

I pushed up on the balls of my feet, trying to see over

heads what was happening. "How did you even meet Jason?"

"My father freaked out about the violence in our neighborhood, he got me a working transfer this year to VH. I met Freddie and Jason at the mall. Jason and I hooked up. But the problems with Carlos . . . I was scared.

"I tried to stop seeing Jason for a while until things cooled down. He kept having Freddie try and set up a meeting between us . . . so Carlos thinks I'm dating Freddie."

I met her gaze. "And now you're pregnant."

Her eyes widened. "Jason told you."

I didn't have time to deny it. Someone rushed into the hallway, grabbing Dominique.

Carlos.

Sweat ran down his forehead. Blood was smeared around his busted lip.

"*Let go,*" Dominique whispered.

He pushed her down. She fell through the open doorway into the bedroom. "Get up!" he yelled.

"Leave her alone!" I stepped into the room, reached for her. *Where's Anthony? Jason?*

Carlos shoved something hard against my gut. "Help her up, and walk."

I swallowed and looked down.

Carlos held a gun to my stomach.

"Don't even think about screaming," Carlos said in my ear. "I'll pull this trigger on you. I don't give a shit right now. I just wanna talk to Dominique."

I helped Dominique to her feet. "So talk to her."

"Not here."

"Get away from them." Jason wrenched Carlos's arm from behind.

Carlos whirled.

"No!" I shouted. He didn't see the gun.

Carlos slammed the weapon against Jason's face, hitting once, twice. Jason crumpled to the floor.

"Jason!" Terror shot through my blood. I tried to push Carlos away from my brother, but at the same time Carlos shoved me. I fell onto the bed. I rose up and the gun was pushed toward my face.

My heart pounded as I stared at the nose of the gun.

"Don't make me pull the trigger. Now *move*."

I jerked my head in a nod, then got to my feet. Carlos held on to Dominique's arm and led us through a sliding glass door on the other side of the bedroom. The gun was loaded. I'd seen it in a sign, firing shots. I just didn't know who would be on the receiving end. Now I wondered if it might be me.

I glanced back at Jason. Blood dripped from his head. And I looked straight ahead. I had to get Carlos away from my brother.

We walked out onto the lawn. Kids were taking off. Sirens crooned in the distance.

"Move!" Carlos held the gun on me, discreetly tucked under his jacket sleeve, his other hand gripped around Dominique's arm.

I saw where we were headed. Anthony's Chevelle.

"Grab the hide-a-key under the front tire," he ordered.

I did as he said. I tried to move slowly, but he yanked Dominique's hair. She cried out.

"Don't mess with me. Move your ass faster."

I did. My hands shook, making it difficult to get the key in the lock.

"Get behind the wheel."

I slid into the driver's seat. He and Dominique got in the back.

I had to scoot all the way to the edge of the seat in order to reach the gas pedal. I pumped it just like I'd seen Anthony do before and turned the ignition. The loud rumble of the engine shook underneath me, and I knew Anthony heard. He'd know the sound of his car. He'd come right away.

Carlos knocked the back of my seat. "Drive!"

Pushing on the gas pedal, I drove.

Carlos made me take the highway out of town. I glanced at my cell phone beside me. It was turned off. If I could manage to slip it inside my pocket . . .

"I loved you, Dominique. And you just leave me for somebody else. Some punk-ass white boy."

A small measure of relief seeped inside me. Carlos still believed Dominique was seeing Freddie. Jason was safe for now. In a quick movement, I snatched the cell and stuffed it into my sweatshirt pocket.

"You hurt me, Carlos."

"I loved you and you cut out my heart by leaving *me*!"

We drove along the ocean until Carlos said, "Turn here."

My heart raced as I continued to drive straight.

The gun tip was knocked into my neck. I hunched with pain and the car swerved.

"I said to fuckin' turn."

Trembling, I took the next turnoff to the beach.

35. The Beach

I couldn't let go of the steering wheel. I was parked in the beach parking lot. The sound of the waves crashing onshore echoed in my head like a lethal threat.

Carlos yelled at me. "Get out of the car!"

It felt like something pressed against the center of my chest. "I can't . . ." I whispered.

He grabbed my wrist and yanked. I held on to the steering wheel as hard as I could, but Carlos was just too strong. He tore my grip away, his fingers bruising my wrist.

I fell onto the cement, grains of sand scraped against my palms. My cell phone dropped, clattering against the concrete. I shifted up onto my hands and knees. Carlos shoved my butt with his foot and pushed. I crawled onto the sand.

I can't believe this is happening.

"Move, Kara! What the hell's the matter with you!"

I wanted to scream, "You!" But my throat was so tight it was too difficult to speak.

Dominique cried from somewhere behind me. The rumble of the waves crashing onto the shore grew louder. I moved slowly, trying to breathe. It was like sucking air through a straw.

I concentrated on moving one arm, one knee forward. Then the other. The soft spray of salty water on my face. The taste of it on my lips. The cold air, blowing my hair back into the wild wind.

"Daddy," I whispered into the wind and remembered the day of the accident . . .

My pulse roared in my ears along with the rumble of thunder that vibrated above us in the boat. The rain pelted us like tiny rocks. I held tight to the handrail. Dad rushed us to the shore.

"No!" Dad yelled. "Damn it, hold on!"

And then we were in the air, tilting. My hands slid away from the handle.

I screamed as I flew. Nothing but air surrounded me.

"Kara!"

I slammed into the ocean. Shock. Ice. Salt water clogged my mouth.

My arms struggling through thick, freezing water. Kelp tangled around my limbs. My life jacket forced me toward the surface.

Daddy!

He floated underwater. I could barely make him out in the

darkness. His hand reached for mine, his hair floating around his face. I reached out. Our fingers brushed, then gripped.

A current rushed us apart, my arms frantic, reaching for him as I floated straight up. My head hit something hard.

The boat.

Daddy . . .

Tears ran down my face. I hadn't been able to hold on to him. I'd been so afraid. If I'd been stronger, braver, maybe I could have done more. Reached out, swam toward him. Anything more. All I kept thinking about was how he'd been alone. How he could no longer hold his breath. He must have been terrified. *Oh, Daddy.* My heart squeezed and broke all over again.

"You remember when we made love here the first time," Carlos yelled from behind me.

"Yesss," Dominique cried back.

"Why wouldn't you just do as I say? Why did you have to fight with me all the time?"

"Carlos, please stop! Just let us go. I'll do whatever you say."

"Oh, so now you want me back? Is that what you want? Tell me you want me back!"

I swallowed hard past the thickness in my throat. When I'd first awoke in the hospital after the accident, I'd told Jason and Mom what I'd seen. Everyone told me I'd been dreaming . . .

A man had walked in front of the foot of my hospital bed. He stopped and turned his attention toward me. Empty. No other word to describe the look in his eyes. Then he continued on and walked straight through the door.

Fear hit me like a slap. My body jerked.

Mom! Dad!

I couldn't scream. I remained frozen. My chest hurt and tears sprung to my eyes. I saw a shadow move behind the curtain to my right.

Helplessly, I sat there, waiting for the shadow to move . . .

The curtain began to slowly slide open. I gripped the bed bars on either side of me.

The curtain slid all the way back and I couldn't move. I couldn't breathe . . .

"Daddy?" My voice was raw, barely a whisper.

He stood there, pale, almost translucent. He waved. Waved to me as if saying hello or good-bye. I didn't know. Until he turned and walked away . . . through the wall.

"No, Daddy . . . come back!" I cried, shudders wracking my aching body. Then I screamed.

"I'm never letting you go, Dominique." Carlos's voice, thick with tears, brought me back. "Never!"

With slow movements, I pushed myself to my feet. My body was still so heavy. A painful constriction in my chest. My heart pounded.

When Carlos saw me back on my feet, the gun that was at his side jerked up. He swung the weapon back and forth between Dominique and me.

I couldn't stop the tears running down my face. All of us were crying. Crying for what was happening, crying that maybe we wouldn't make it off this beach alive.

Think, Kara. Think what to do.

My hands clenched at my sides. The signs had led me here. I couldn't just give up like I had after losing my father.

Fight, mi'ja.

With one shot, my life could be taken away. Sometimes I thought that if I'd been the one to die that day instead of Dad, everyone would have been happier. Mom and Jason. Now, standing in the face of it, I knew I didn't want to die. Surviving that day was a miracle. A gift. I wanted a future. I wanted a chance to live.

Sobs were shuddering through Carlos's body. He swiped his hand across his mouth. "But you'll never take me back, will you? You'll just say what I want to hear, then run to the cops."

Dominique shook her head. "No, I won't. I—"

"Liar!" His eyes seemed to go dead. He'd made a decision. "It's over."

"Carlos, d-don't do this," I stammered, trembling from the cold. From the fear. "Think of Anthony. He loves you. If you hurt us, you'll go to jail. What will he think?"

"Nah, Anthony loved Pedro. When he died, everything changed! All I had was Dominique. Now she's gone."

"Carlos, I'm not gone. *Please.*"

"Yeah, you are. You're already gone."

Carlos cocked the gun and aimed it at Dominique.

Time shifted to fast-forward. And it was like a key turning inside a lock, a click echoing in my head. I grabbed Dominique's hand.

I squeezed tight and pulled her toward the ocean.

Carlos screamed and fired a shot.

Sand sprayed at our feet where the bullet hit. We ran as fast as we could toward the water, the sand uneven clumps beneath our feet. Tears mixed with sweat on my face. Terror was like an electric current through my body, pushing me to get away from Carlos and the gun.

Have to hide. In the waves. Till the bullets run out.

The water was like liquid ice. I sucked in a breath. My stiff fingers clenched onto Dominique's hand.

"Don't let go!" I told her.

Someone yelled behind us. Had to be Carlos. I wasn't sure. The water rushed past our waists. A wave crashed over our shoulders. Dominique lost her footing and fell into the dark water.

I squeezed tight, gripped her arm with my other hand, digging my shoes into the sinking sand, and pulled her to her feet. Another wave plowed over us. Water stinging my eyes. I spit water out of my mouth, shook my head to get wet clumps of hair out of my face.

"Kara!" A distant yell. Was it inside my head?

I glanced back. My teeth chattered.

Anthony. He ran toward his brother and tackled him. The brothers smashed into the water.

My chest squeezed. I tried to turn toward the shore with Dominique. My wet clothes weighed me down.

Two shots fired. *No!*

A wave slammed over us. I lost my balance, and I was floating in the liquid darkness. Water clogged my ears. Burned my eyes. Rushed into my mouth, choking me. I could feel Dominique's hand slipping away.

Don't let go, mi'ja. *Hold tight.*

The current shoved us deeper into the ocean, kelp tangled around our arms.

Losing air. My lungs would burst any second.

Still, I wouldn't let go. I gripped her hand, and she did mine.

Someone grabbed my other hand. I held tight as I was pulled toward the shore, Dominique still with me.

My knees shoved against the bottom. Then the hand let go and I crawled toward shore. Coughing. Gagging up seawater. Chills shuddered through my body. Tiny needles danced underneath my skin.

Anthony was there, sliding our arms around his shoulders, helping us to dry sand, where we all collapsed.

He's okay. I glanced at Dominique. She spat up water, but she was conscious against the sand.

Anthony rushed to me on his knees, cradled my head with his hand. The wind blew his hair away from his face. I shook with harsh chills.

"Kara, an ambulance is coming. It'll be okay." He started unbuttoning my soaked sweater.

"Carlos . . . ?"

"He's okay."

"You—you came after me." My voice was rough, broken.

"Always."

"I. Didn't. Let go."

"What?"

My teeth knocked together. Beads of water slid down my face. "Of Dom-Dominique. You. Held tight . . . when you grabbed my hand . . . pulled us out. The water."

He tugged my sweater off. "I didn't pull you out. I saw you already crawling up the shore."

I heard the sirens come closer.

"They're here," he said. "They'll get you warm, damn it." He lifted his head and shouted, "Here! Over here!"

"Didn't . . . grab my hand . . . in the water?"

He shook his head. "No, Kara. Try not to talk."

The medics rushed to us. They laid me back on the sand, and I stared up at the dark sky. Stars winked in and out behind blankets of fog. An oxygen mask was placed over my mouth and nose as soaked clothes were pulled from my skin.

If it hadn't been Anthony . . .

36. Nothing Changes

"How's Carlos?"

"It's a thigh shot, tore his muscle up. He'll be here a couple of days, then . . . jail until a hearing."

"I'm so sorry."

Anthony swore, walked away. We were in the ER. The doctor had checked me out, but I still wore a hospital gown and medic pants. They'd had to get me out of my wet clothes to keep me from going into shock or hypothermia. I'd answered questions from the police about what had happened at the party and the beach.

"Kara, I'm the one who's sorry." He shoved his hands through his hair. Gray sweats rode low on his hips. He was shirtless under his flannel. The medic had ordered him out of his wet clothes. He had a bruise on his right cheekbone from the fight, and another on his chin. "I'm sorry my brother did this. He nearly killed you."

"It's not your fault."

He shook his head. "Not so sure about that."

My heart raced with his uncertainty. "Believe it." I licked my dry lips. I still tasted salt. Grains of sand were buried in my hair and other undesirable places. "Anthony, how did you know?"

He looked at me. "Know what?"

"Where Carlos had taken us?"

He shrugged. "A hunch. I knew Carlos had taken Dominique there a lot. After I knocked out Freddie—"

My mouth dropped open. "You knocked him out?"

A look of disgust flickered across his face. "His punk ass deserved it. Then I'd found Jason in the bedroom. He'd said Carlos had been with you and Dom. I'd heard my car. I grabbed a friend's ride and took off."

"A pretty good hunch."

He blew out a breath, but he wouldn't meet my eyes. "Yeah. I outran your brother to the car, he could barely walk, but I had to get to you. Didn't know what Carlos was thinking. I knew he had a quick temper, been having trouble after Dominique broke things off, but I never thought he was capable of *this.*"

Just then my mother stepped into the room, Jason behind her, holding a duffel bag. He had a bandage on his forehead with bruising around his right eye.

Mom's face was pale, her hair down and wild. "Oh my God, Kara." She ran to me, wrapped her arms around me, and began to cry. Her subtle perfume wrapped around me, comforting me. "My baby. I love you."

"Mom, I'm okay." I swallowed past a lump in my throat. I didn't remember Mom crying since Dad, and never like this. Her tears had always been quiet and controlled. "I love you too." I heard Jason and Anthony talking, watched as they grabbed hands and patted shoulders. Things were good with them.

"If anything happened to you . . ." Suddenly she swung away toward Anthony so fast I nearly fell forward. She pushed him with her open hands. "And *you*."

My eyes snapped wide. "Mom!"

She shoved him again with two hands. Anthony stepped back, letting her. "*You* and your crazy brother nearly getting my baby killed."

"Mom, take it easy." Jason grabbed her shoulders, holding her back.

Anthony raised his hands in a gesture of surrender. "I'm sorry, Mrs. Martinez . . ."

"Katherine, let's try to stay calm."

Shock rippled through my body. I slowly turned toward the doorway as if bracing myself to face the boogeyman.

Dr. Hathaway stood there with her hair neatly in a bun, her hands folded in front of her. Despite the late hour, she was as calm and put together as I'd always seen her.

"*Sorry?*" Mom continued to yell. "Sorry won't cut it. Your brother is going away for a long time. I will personally see to it. If I could, I'd send you away with him."

"I never wanted Kara hurt. If he had . . ." Anthony gestured with his hand, shook his head. His expression was so sad with regret, my chest hurt.

"Do you know what I've been through with Kara since the accident that took her father? That nearly took her life?"

I straightened, glancing cautiously at Dr. Hathaway. "Mom, don't do this."

"It changed all of our lives. Then she wakes up screaming about ghosts walking through walls. Saying that she sees awful images on people. Her mind was not right after the accident. She thinks I don't know that she still suffers from nightmares and headaches."

She's known all along.

Anthony glanced at me, then at my mom.

I shut my eyes as everything inside began to crumble. "No, *don't do this.*" I covered my hands with my face. In just a few moments she could crush me with the past, leaving me to wish I'd never trusted her, never told her what I'd seen those first few days after the accident.

"I had to put her in hospitals, take her to doctors for years, because she was emotionally distraught over losing her father. And now when she's finally getting better, a normal life, you come around and take all I've done and throw it out the window. Drag her down with your gang lifestyle."

Anthony rubbed his hand through his hair, his eyes glossy. "I never wanted Kara hurt. I care about her too much." His Adam's apple moved in his throat as if it was difficult to swallow. "I'm sorry." He strode past Dr. Hathaway and out of the room.

Tears slid down my face as I watched him go.

Mom turned back, reached for me. "It's okay, baby. Everything will be okay."

I pushed her away with what little strength I had. "I'm not a baby. I'm grown, Mom. How could you tell him all that?"

"Tell her what you're feeling, Katherine." Dr. Hathaway's irritatingly calm voice bullied her way into our family drama.

Mom threw her hands up in the air. "You're so grown that you sneak out of the house? You disobey me. You run around town with gang members? You almost drown again!" Her voice broke. "Dr. Hathaway has secured you a stay at Jameson. I think you need some time away."

My heart squeezed. My shoulders sagged. I didn't even have enough emotion to cry anymore. To fight against the both of them. I was on my way to Jameson. Back on medication. Back to a world with no privacy. No freedom. To a place that dampened my spirit and left me cold. A place filled with people who would continue to tell me I was sick and that I needed to get better, people who would never listen to the truth.

"No, Mom. That's not going to happen."

We both looked at Jason. He moved to put his arm around me. He ignored Dr. Hathaway and met Mom's eyes. "I've got my own apartment. It's small. But I'm taking Kara home with me if you're sending her to Jameson. I'm not letting you do this to her again. She's not sick, Mom." He shook his head. "She's just not."

Warmth flooded through me. I looked at my brother with

tears running down my cheeks. He shifted his eyes to me and gave me a small smile of reassurance.

"Katherine, you are the parent," Dr. Hathaway said. "Kara needs your help to get better. We can go straight to Jameson tonight and send her things tomorrow."

Mom's hands were fisted at her sides as she stared at us. Her eyes watered. She was shaking so hard, I was worried she might explode.

"Katherine—"

Without turning, Mom said, "Just shut up, Dr. Hathaway."

Dr. Hathaway fiddled with the scarf at her throat. "Well."

To me, Mom said, "Fine. If that's the way it's going to be, I will check you out." She walked out of the room.

I fell back on the bed, dizzy.

Jason hovered over me, his face etched with concern. "Kara, are you okay? Do you need a doctor?"

"God, no." I shook my head, suddenly laughing. "I'm okay. I'm really okay."

37. Good Dreams

After I changed into the clothes that Mom had brought, I walked out of the ER with Jason. Dr. Hathaway had strode off. Mom was gone. I didn't know what to think. I didn't know what it meant to have both of us stand against her. Mom had so much pride, so much stubbornness.

"What do I do now?" I asked Jason.

"Let Mom cool off, stay at my place tonight. I meant it, Kara. If Mom tries to send you away, you can live with me. You'll be eighteen before you know it."

I blinked back tears. It felt really good to have someone in the family by my side. To have my brother back. "But what about Dominique, the baby. Is she okay?"

His expression went serious. "So you know."

I nodded.

"Yeah, she and the baby checked out fine. I'm going to take care of the baby, and Dominique, if she'll let me. She's eighteen, but we have to work it out with her parents. We have to work out a lot of things. I know the type of father Dad was to us. He set an example and always told me to follow through with my responsibility. We'll find out if I can make him proud."

My brother was young, but I could already tell he was ready to take this on. To do his best even though being a father had to be terrifying. Things were no longer the same with us, but they were heading for the better. I could feel it.

"You will," I said. "You'll make him proud."

The two of us went home to Jason's one-room loft. He gave me his mattress on the floor, and he took the floor with a sleeping bag. I called Mom. She didn't answer. I left a message and told her where I was staying for the night. I tried Anthony and got his voice mail too.

Staring at the ceiling, I replayed the night in my head. The beach, the ocean, the hand that I had thought helped me out of the water. Or had it just been my imagination? Everything had been so chaotic. I wasn't so sure anymore . . .

Exhaustion won out and my eyes drifted shut.

I was back on the boat, but I wasn't eleven. I was seventeen, and Dad was steering. My heart pounded. I whipped my head around. The ocean was calm. The sun blared down on us like a beautiful gem. Not a cloud in sight. The colors of the sky were bright blue and sunset pink, the ocean glittering like diamonds.

"Okay, *mi'ja*?"

"Dad?"

He laughed. "Who else? Beautiful weather today. Too bad Mamacita and Jason didn't come."

I frowned. Something was weird, but I couldn't put my finger on it. I just nodded. "Yeah, they're missing out."

"You wanna take the wheel?"

I smiled. "Really?"

"Yeah, yeah. Come on." Dad slowed the boat, and I stepped to him.

I took the steering and he accelerated the boat. "This is cool."

"Hey, watch out for that dolphin!"

There wasn't a sea animal in sight. "Dad, stop."

He laughed. "I think I'll make tacos tonight. Sound good?"

"Sounds great. I haven't had your tacos in forever."

"What do you mean? I just made them last week."

"Last week?" I frowned.

"Yeah. Here, let's go faster." He stood beside me and slipped his arm over my shoulder. I could smell his musky aftershave.

A feeling of warmth stirred in my chest. "Dad, I love you."

"I love you, *mi'ja*."

The dream shifted.

It was Mom and me. She painted her toenails while I played with her makeup. She smiled and started painting my small toes. I was a little girl, and we giggled together.

I was older as I rode my bike. I crashed and fell in the driveway. Mom ran to me, picked me up, and checked my knee. She washed away the blood and dirt and bandaged the scrape, then held me as I sniffled and cried.

Sick with the flu, Mom held my hair back as I got sick. She helped me to the bed, covered me up, and placed a cool rag on my head. I slept, and when I woke Mom was sleeping in a chair, watching over me through the night.

After the accident, I had a nightmare at home. I sat up, shoved the covers back, my heart racing. Mom. I wanted Mom. I walked in the dark to her room, and I found her crying.

She was sobbing in heart-wrenching pain. Her shoulders shuddered. Her hands covered her face. She rocked back and forth in excruciating grief.

"Roberto," she cried. "Oh, Roberto. What am I going to do without you?"

38. The Friend

Sunday morning, I awoke with so many aches and pains I felt like I'd survived an all-out brawl. My eyes were red-rimmed and grainy. My throat was raw when I swallowed. I got up slowly and noticed Jason was gone. I raised a hand to my drumming head. *Oh damn, my head feels like it might fall off.*

I stumbled over to the kitchen, where Jason left a note saying that he'd gone to see Dominique and her parents. I tried calling Anthony again, and still got his voice mail.

"It's me . . ." I cleared my throat. "I just want to see how you are. And Carlos." I had nothing else to say. He probably never wanted to see me again. Why would he, after learning his girlfriend had been sent to a mental facility for claiming to see ghosts and weird images on people?

I hung up.

Sadly, my brother wasn't a coffee drinker. One lonely can of Coke sat in the fridge. I scooped it up, pulled the tab, and guzzled down three fast gulps. Instant brain freeze. I winced, then covered my mouth over a carbonated belch.

Jason's computer sat on a counter in the small kitchen nook. Last night he'd told me he just had dial-up. I leaned against the counter—no stools yet—and booted up his laptop. A few lazy minutes of logging onto the Net and then I checked my blog.

Several comments. The usual few telling me I was a fake, others that were supportive. I spotted the latest single-word comments from anonymous:

> anonymous said . . .
> help

> anonymous said . . .
> forgive

I scrolled down to my previous entries with single-word comments. *Friend. Secret. Pain.*

My hand tightened on the edge of the counter. *Why hadn't I pieced these comments together before?*

Logging on, I wrote a quick blog entry.

Then, after carefully clearing out the laptop's history, I shut it down, took a fast shower, dressed, and headed out the door.

Anonymous friend, I know who you are. We need to talk. I value our friendship. I'm on my way to you.

—Sign Seer

39. Hands

Carmen let me into the house. Mr. and Mrs. Salazar were out shopping. I found Danielle in her room. She was huddled on the floor, rocking forward and back. Papers all around. Drawings. Of hands.

"Danielle?" I said her name quietly. She was alone in her room, and I was almost afraid to intrude.

She had her arms around her bent knees. She shook her head. Her hair flowed around her legs like wavy vines. It was as if she was staring into some empty place no one else could see. I had the urge to move my hand into the space just to be sure something wasn't there.

"I can't get them right," she said.

"What right?" I went to step forward, but I didn't want to step on any of her beautiful work.

I kneeled just on the edges. The papers were like a barrier around her that no one could penetrate. I picked up a page and saw the hands of a man splayed out. I set it down and picked up another.

I looked closely at another, and another.

They were all of the same hands.

"Whose hands are these?"

"His."

"Whose?" I watched her continue to rock. "Danielle . . . please, tell me."

"My parents' best friend. The man who died."

She's still grieving. "It's okay, Danielle. I'll get your sister or call your mom."

Her eyes finally shifted to mine. I had a moment to think, *I've never seen her eyes so full of emotion, so intense,* before she said, "*No.* I can't. Can't tell her." A tear ran down her cheek.

My pulse sped up. "What can't you tell her?"

She looked back into that empty space and started to rock faster.

Pushing the drawings aside, I made a path to her. Placing my hands on her shoulders to stop her movement, I looked into her eyes. "You're my best friend. You can tell me anything. You can trust me with your secrets."

I think she knew I spoke the truth. This was the first time I'd ever told her this. The first time I was breaking our silent vow of friendship not to go deeper than we'd been comfortable with all this time.

I was asking her to share her secrets.

Her eyes squeezed shut. "H-he touched me."

The crying didn't stop for what seemed like forever. She cried as if telling the secret broke the dam that was holding her together. Danielle had always been the stronger one. She'd been the brave one who'd say what was on her mind. The one not afraid to jump in after her sister when Carmen was facing off with Josie. The one always wanting to protect her family . . .

I was supposed to be able to follow the signs and pay attention to signals others ignored. And here I hadn't even known my best friend had been hurting and hiding a painful secret. Yeah, I'd known *something* was going on with her, but I'd been too scared to ask her what. Too afraid that if she shared with me, I'd have to do the same.

We were lying across from each other on the floor among the pieces of paper. The sketches crunched under our legs as we shifted.

"It happened a few times." Her voice was soft, just over a whisper. "Years would go by before he'd have another opportunity. I just remember feeling dirty. Still do. I mean, I was only five the first time and I didn't really understand, and when he told me not to tell, I didn't."

She blinked eyes that were red and glossy. "When I got older, it was stolen touches almost right out in the open, in front of everyone. It makes me *sick* to remember. I'll go months without even thinking about it, like it happened to someone else, but then something would make me remember . . . a show on TV. My parents mentioning his name. And I'm back . . . five again."

I didn't interrupt her or ask questions. I could never relate to the sexual abuse Danielle had gone through, but I knew how a tragic memory could take you back to where you re-lived it again and again. How many times had Danielle played it through in her mind?

Hundreds? Too many to count? A shudder ran through me just thinking about it.

I licked my lips. "Danielle . . . you need to tell your parents."

She shook her head. "I told you, I can't. It'll kill my parents. They'll blame themselves."

"Like you blame yourself?"

She didn't answer.

"You've held this in for years . . . and it's hurting *you*. I know what it's like holding a secret in for too long. It eats inside of you like a disease. He's gone now, he can't hurt you again."

"I know. Only in my head."

I swallowed. "And that's why it's time to tell."

She shut her eyes. "What if they think I'm dirty?" she whispered. Tears slipped across the bridge of her nose and down to one of the drawings. "What if they look at me different?

"What if . . . they don't believe me?"

I was almost afraid to answer. I wanted to tell her they would look at her the same as they always had. I wanted to re-assure her so she'd just take the first step to try to heal. But hadn't my mom and my brother looked at me with fear in their eyes when I told them what I'd seen in the hospital, and about the signs?

No, my family hadn't believed me, and it had scarred something inside of me.

"Sometimes," I said, "you have to take a chance on the what-ifs. I know it won't be easy. But I have this theory."

Her eyes opened.

"That when you tell a secret that's been inside you for so long, it feels really good to finally release it." I sighed. I was about to break one of my coveted Life Rules by telling her everything. "You've read my blog."

She nodded, watching me carefully. "I'm sorry about the notes."

I nodded. I believed her.

"It's just, I'd never been more afraid to ask you about your secret. Because if you had told me . . . then maybe I'd finally tell mine. It sounds stupid, but it's *so* hard, Kara. I don't think I can tell them."

"I know it's hard. I'm ready to tell you mine . . . then we'll see."

She nodded, her face scraping against a drawing.

"When I was eleven, I died for eleven minutes. I went out on a boat with my father . . ."

40. Unbroken

went home with tears still in my eyes. Danielle had told her parents while I held her hand. It had been painful seeing everyone cry and hold one another. I slipped up to her room when Danielle fell asleep in her mother's arms, got what I needed, then left. I will forever remember how Danielle's secret had crushed the family, then brought them together with emotional support. The Salazar family had a strong bond that I couldn't ever imagine being broken.

I wondered if our family could ever be strong again like we had been when Dad was alive.

The house was dark when I walked in. The shades had yet to be opened. A cup and a bowl sat on the kitchen counter. Mom's coat and purse were on the floor.

In the living room, a blanket was splayed on the couch, the pillows flat and scattered.

My gut tight, I opened the garage door. Mom's car was parked inside. She was home. I texted Jason. I told him to get home now.

Before I went upstairs, I went to the fireplace. I took the drawing of the hands from my tote. They rustled as I pulled them out. The edges were bent, some of the pages crinkled. Opening the glass doors, I tossed them into the fireplace, made sure the flue was opened, and lit the pages with an electric lighter.

For you, Danielle.

I shut the glass doors and watched each page swallowed up by yellow flames. I hadn't seen a forewarning sign on my best friend that told me she was hurting. I'd seen only the real-life signs that I ignored. Now I hoped I could do this one small thing for her, and try to be a better friend, who wasn't afraid of her own secrets.

Taking a breath, I straightened and walked up the staircase. My bedroom door was open. Mom lay slouched against my pillows on my bed. Her eyes were closed. I watched her chest slowly rise, up and down. Wadded-up tissues lay against her lap. One of the biggest surprises was Faith cuddled at the foot of the bed.

My secret laundry bag and clothes were scattered on the floor. My closet open with clothes pushed together and hangers poking out. My thermos was out and standing up on my carpet. My iMac was on, but it looked like she couldn't get past my encrypted password. The desk drawers were open to varying degrees. Papers and books were scattered about.

All my note cards from previous signs were spread around the carpet.

My pulse sped up at the sight of them even though I knew she wouldn't understand what they were to me.

I wanted to be angry that she went through my things. But I was more shocked by what was going on with her. Here was my strong, independent mother, looking so fragile.

Defeated.

"Mom?"

She awoke. Her green eyes were bloodshot and swollen. She shifted on my pillows and rubbed at her neck with a pained expression. She looked around my room and saw the mess she had made.

"I wanted to know all your secrets," she said, her voice husky with emotion. "I tried. And I failed."

I stayed at the front of the room. I was afraid to go to her, to touch her. I'd never seen Mom like this. I always saw her as a leader. Someone strong and sure of herself. Never afraid. And now . . .

Guilt weighed heavy on my shoulders. Was this all my fault?

"After the accident, after Rob passed, I knew all that mattered was getting you better. Taking care of you and Jason and holding this family together. Look at us now. Oh damn, I screwed up."

What could I say? It's okay? Our broken family wasn't

okay, but we couldn't put it all on Mom's shoulders. When she didn't believe me about the signs, I was crushed. I had needed her more than ever, but Mom lived in the real world. Sometimes she only saw things in black and white. The signs she couldn't see weren't possible to her. I had accepted that, but in the process I'd forgotten all the good that we had shared before the accident.

I'd lost Dad to death. I didn't want to lose the family I still had left to fear and old wounds. I had to forgive her for not believing me. I had to accept that she never would because that's who she was. I loved her anyway.

"It's not all your fault." I took a hesitant step forward. "Jason and I have made some not-so-great decisions too. It's like the more you tried to keep us together, the more we all pushed each other away."

"That stubborn Martinez blood." She tried to smile but didn't quite pull it off. "I miss your father. He always knew the right thing to say, to make us laugh. I wanted things to stay the same with the three of us. But missing him made it too hard. I pushed everything that reminded me of him away. Music, his clothes, even his favorite things, the food he loved. Even the culture that your father loved and who we all are. I just couldn't bear it. The harder I tried to pull us together, the more I lost control. I could see I was losing you both completely."

I heard the front door open and close, then Jason walking around downstairs. I imagined his face in shock at the disarray of the house. His heavy steps ran up the stairs. He stopped at my room, a hand on the doorjamb.

His eyes were wide, his cheeks flushed. "What's going on?"

"Mom needs us," I said.

Jason blew out a breath. "She's got us."

That day we sat down as a family and talked. Really talked. I told Mom I'd feared her and Dr. Hathaway for a long time, and that I didn't need sessions anymore. What I needed was for her to believe that I was okay, and that I was old enough to make my own decisions.

No, I didn't mention again what I saw in the hospital after the accident. Or the signs I still see today. Mom would never be ready for that. But I wanted her to realize I was no longer that same little girl who awoke terrified in a hospital bed.

Mom said she'd never stop worrying; she was my mother, after all, but she believed Dr. Hathaway was no longer needed. That maybe in her own way, she'd been clinging to Dr. Hathaway for her own insecurities.

It was more than I ever thought she'd admit. I thought it better to bring up Anthony another time. I wasn't quite sure if he still would be a part of my life. I did mention the pink clothes. I couldn't stop myself. She actually smiled and said she knew. No more pink.

When she asked Jason if he'd consider moving back home until he was really ready to move out, he dropped his news.

The baby news.

There was shock, and yelling on both sides, but in the end Mom calmed down enough to discuss his plans and options. She was far from happy, but she wasn't turning her back on him. I think she was surprised by how mature he was about what he was prepared to do for the sake of the baby. She wanted to meet Dominique, have her over for dinner.

Jason's response? "If you promise you won't cook."

She'd suggested a Mexican menu.

We all laughed a little, breaking the heavy tension in the room.

I hoped it was the first family laugh in a long line of many.

41. Feather Man

Two days later, Anthony stood at my front door. He held Faith, stroking her damp hair.

"I didn't hear your car," I said, fingering my Rubik's Cube.

The heat wave had gone. The pitter-patter of raindrops landed behind him. His hair was wet, his flannel jacket spotted with dark drops. His handsome face still had bruises. He set Faith down and shoved his hands into the pockets of his jeans. Faith settled on the doormat. Mom had snapped back to her senses—Faith was confined to the outdoors again.

Anthony's mouth tilted up on one side. "Parked down the street. Habit." He shrugged. "Have time to talk?"

"Kara, who is it?"

I tensed, and I could see Anthony shift, pull his shoulders back as if readying for battle.

Mom halted beside me. "Oh. You have company."

"Hello, Mrs. Martinez," Anthony said. His expression was clear, without any signs of anger or bad feelings from their last encounter.

"Hello."

An uncomfortable moment of silence stretched between us. I don't know what I was waiting for. I couldn't imagine her jumping out and shoving him again.

I cleared my throat. "I'm just going to talk to Anthony for a bit."

"Fine." Then with a small smile she said, "*Hace frío. Usa tu chaqueta.*"

I smiled. I'd thought Mom didn't speak Spanish, but she knew it well. She'd admitted she was pretty rusty, but she'd work on helping me learn because I wanted to so badly.

"*Sí, mamá.*" Sighing with relief, I grabbed my jacket and stepped out, shutting the door behind me. Mom had been trying not to make my decisions for me. Including having Anthony in my life. *If* he still wanted to be. She admitted she couldn't blame him for his brother's actions. For her, it was difficult. But at least she was doing her best. I debated whether to stay under the porch roof, then jogged toward the tree on our lawn for more privacy.

Anthony walked behind me, not in any hurry.

This was it. He had come to end our relationship. My chest ached already from the thought of having him this close to me only to lose him. I leaned against the tree trunk. He stood before me, but not too close. The air was crisp, and I could smell the damp grass and leaves. A cold drop of rain fell onto my cheek from the leaves above me, then another.

He tapped the cube with his finger. "You solved it again."

I lifted the puzzle. Some of the cubes were loose, and it had a ton of scratches on the surface. "My dad gave me this cube. It helps me sort things out in my head."

"Guess you've been doing a lot of thinking."

I smiled. "Guess so." Yeah, I'd been doing a lot of thinking and writing. I'd finally gotten the guts to write about the loss of my dad for my English essay. How it had changed my family, and how now we were finally ready to heal.

"I've had some time on my hands too." He pulled his cell phone from his front pocket, flipped it open, and pressed a couple of buttons. He shifted the screen toward me.

Tetris score: Level 12, 34,543.

My mouth opened slightly as I pulled out my phone from my pants pocket and showed him my score.

Level 12, 34,543.

"That is . . ." he said.

"So weird," I finished for him.

His eyebrows pulled together. "Is it true . . . what your mom said at the hospital?"

My throat grew thick as I shut my phone and slipped it back in my pocket. I swallowed hard, turning the cube in my hands. "Pretty much. What she doesn't know is that I still see the images on people." I'd decided I could only share the secret with the people I felt I could trust and who could handle it. At the moment, that was Danielle and Anthony. Jason had a lot going on right now. And Mom just wouldn't be able to deal. She was too settled in reality.

~~Life Rule: Mom needed her reality.~~

I almost forgot, no more Life Rules. Sometimes . . . rules were meant to be broken.

"I don't understand," he said, studying my face.

I looked down at my tennis shoes, brushing against the blades of wet grass and yellowish leaves. "Maybe you're not meant to."

"Kara, I want to try."

I told him about waking in the hospital after the boat accident, and what I'd seen. How no one had believed me. And the signs I had finally learned to follow. My secret blog. The gun puzzle that led to the party and the beach.

"I'm sorry I didn't tell you about the sign on Carlos. First, I thought you wouldn't believe me. Second, I had no idea what the image meant." I blew out a breath. "It's complicated."

Silence stretched between us as he took it all in. I didn't dare look him in the eyes. But I knew I couldn't be frightened anymore. I took one of the biggest stands in my life on the beach that night. It was time to face my fears instead of running from them.

I looked at him.

He was watching me. "Images on people's chests."

I nodded.

"And you help people."

I rolled my shoulder. "I try . . ."

"See?" He lifted a finger in my direction and tapped the air. "Brave."

For some strange reason, my cheeks heated.

"And don't be sorry about Carlos. I'm still trying to tell myself it wasn't my fault what he did. He's my younger brother. He looked up to me and I let him down."

"Just so you know, I don't think his actions are your fault. How is he?"

He shook his head. "Not good. He's under psych evaluation right now. It's going to be tough for my mom, our family. We're just relieved no one else was really hurt." He met my eyes. "Physically, anyway."

I was still afraid to reach out to him. I didn't know where we stood in our relationship. He looked like he wanted to say more, but I didn't want to push him.

"I have dreams." He said it so quickly it took me a moment to comprehend what he'd said.

I frowned. "Me too."

Shoving his damp hair back, he walked away into the light rain and back. A few fresh drops were on his nose and cheek. "No. The kind that don't make sense, all muddled together. Then I see something happen, and it's like déjà vu. I don't know." He waved a hand in the air. Not much agitated Anthony, but this did. "It's all screwed up."

I blinked, not wanting to jump to conclusions. I straightened against the tree, cleared my throat. "Anthony, what are you saying?"

"I don't know what it means, so you're not going to get more than what I'm saying. I try to forget about them most of the time, as if they don't happen." He looked at me. "But when I met you, I couldn't ignore them. The dreams were stronger. Clearer."

And he told me. That he'd seen me in a dream before we met at Dishes. That was why he'd pulled me from the arcade. He'd dream, and he'd know where I'd be next. The pizzeria where I worked, the small girl we'd saved at the taco stand, even what I liked to drink. He'd seen flickers of images of all these things before they happened.

It was truly surreal to listen to the words coming from his mouth. I wanted to literally pinch myself to see if I was dreaming.

"Anthony . . ."

"I tried to forget you, Kara. I tried to stay away because I was scared shitless. But there you were at the party, and I couldn't deny how much I missed you. How good it felt to be with you. I thought I could be with you, and still ignore the dreams."

"Why do you try to ignore them?"

His jaw clenched.

I reached out and put my hand over his wrist. "It's okay if you don't want to say. I understand how hard this is."

"It's just—I'd *seen* Pedro get shot. I'd seen it in my head, but I didn't tell him. Told him to lay low instead. To be careful. He laughed me off. I didn't know if what I saw would come true. Sometimes I remember dreams that don't make any kind of sense. I'd thought . . . Pedro's dream would end up being the same. I'd wanted it to be wrong.

"With you and Carlos, I'd seen a beach. That's how I knew where he'd taken you. That time, I prayed the dream was right."

"You saved us, Anthony. You believed the dream and you followed."

He looked into my eyes, and I smiled. I knew this was hard for Anthony to accept. But part of me realized I was no longer alone. Someone understood. Someone else had a gift.

It hit me in a flash. The sign that was supposed to show on Anthony that never did. The same feeling I'd felt on the Feather Man.

"Damn," he said with a straight face. "Do you know how hard it's going to be trying to make sure you don't get hurt following these signs?"

El padre. El hombre es bueno.

"Of course," I whispered.

His eyebrows lowered a little. "Kara, I'm kidding."

He must have seen something on my face. His face went pale. "What is it? Are you, like, seeing something?"

"The Feather Man. We have to find him." I grabbed his wrist and pulled him down the street. "Hurry!"

The rain strengthened as we drove through town. Anthony's windshield wipers weren't the greatest. I rolled down his window so I could scan the streets. Raindrops stung my cheeks. The streets were wet and quiet except for the heavy showers splattering against the ground.

"I don't know if he has a home to go to," I said to Anthony.

"We could check the shelters."

"That could take hours."

We found him by chance outside the shelter called Sally's Kitchen. There was a line out the door for a hot meal. He stood beneath a ripped yellow umbrella.

I was afraid to go up to him, but Anthony held my hand as he pulled me out into the rain. We walked over to the Feather Man together.

His eyes met mine. He spoke in Spanish: "The man says he is good."

"Who," I asked.

He gripped my arm, and as the rain soaked me to my skin, he gave me a message from my father.

SECRET FATES:
The Sign Seer's Blog

A lot has happened this past week, and I wish I could share more details. What I will tell you is that I solved the "gun" puzzle. I think this one was so difficult for me to solve because it was personal. It involved people I cared about. It involved me.

The entire experience opened my eyes to things I never would have been able to face had I not gone through them.

I learned to speak, even when I'm afraid, and act when needed even when it isn't the safest thing to do. I've finally taken that step to let myself heal for the loss of a loved one.

The Life Rules have been retired. I started them to make my life less complicated, but life is all about complications, especially when following the signs. I'm ready to take on more puzzles, and try to help those I can.

I know there are visitors who read this blog and still think I'm crazy. And you know what? That will always be the case. There are people in life who only see black and white, and then there are those that can see gray, and red, orange, yellow, and blue too.

But most importantly, I'm not alone. I thought I was for so long, but part of me knows it was my own doing by not being brave enough to let people close, by not trusting. I still have my secrets and this blog will always remain anonymous, but knowing I'm strong enough to finally trust others is one sign I will forever follow.

—Sign Seer